An uneasy feeling shifted through her.

Maren approached the clinic door with her K-9, Haven, at her side. As she reached for the handle, Haven spun, facing the street, and let out a series of frantic barks.

Maren knew the tone of her partner's bark.

Haven was alerting to danger. But from where? And who?

Before Maren could formulate an action plan, gunfire rang out. Bullets pelted the building around her, coming within inches of slamming into her and Haven. The clinic doors burst into a shower of glass. Terrified screams echoed from within.

Maren crouched and reined in Haven's leash. Then she hustled them both toward the nearest parked car to use as cover as more bullets peppered the front of the clinic.

* * *

COLORADO K-9 UNIT

Searching for the Truth by Laura Scott
Tracking the Taken Child by Sharon Dunn
Danger in the Rockies by Terri Reed
Protecting the Baby by Jodie Bailey
Fugitive Manhunt by Sharee Stover
Hunting an Arsonist by Jessica R. Patch
Uncovering Explosive Secrets by Maggie K. Black
Unraveling a Crime Ring by Valerie Hansen
Christmas K-9 Security by Lynette Eason & Lenora Worth

Terri Reed writes heartwarming romance and heart-pounding suspense. Her books have appeared on the *New York Times*, *Publishers Weekly* and Amazon bestseller lists, Nielsen's BookScan top fifty, and have been featured in *USA TODAY*. When not writing, she can be found doing agility with her dog. You can visit her online at www.terrireed.com, sign up for her newsletter for exclusive content or email her at terrireedauthor@terrireed.com.

Books by Terri Reed

Love Inspired Suspense

Buried Mountain Secrets
Secret Mountain Hideout
Christmas Protection Detail
Secret Sabotage
Forced to Flee
Forced to Hide
Undercover Christmas Escape
Shielding the Innocent Target
Trained to Protect
Texas Christmas Cover-Up
Pursued on the Run

Mountain Country K-9 Unit

Search and Detect

Dakota K-9 Unit

Standing Watch

Colorado K-9 Unit

Danger in the Rockies

Visit the Author Profile page at LoveInspired.com for more titles.

DANGER IN THE ROCKIES

TERRI REED

Special thanks and acknowledgment are given to Terri Reed for her contribution to the Colorado K-9 Unit miniseries.

Recycling programs for this product may not exist in your area.

ISBN-13: 978-1-335-95775-7

Danger in the Rockies

For questions and comments about the quality of this book, please contact us at CustomerService@Harlequin.com.

Love Inspired
22 Adelaide St. West, 41st Floor
Toronto, Ontario M5H 4E3, Canada
www.LoveInspired.com

HarperCollins Publishers
Macken House, 39/40 Mayor Street Upper,
Dublin 1, D01 C9W8, Ireland
www.HarperCollins.com

Printed in Lithuania

Now faith is the substance of things hoped for,
the evidence of things not seen.
—*Hebrews* 11:1

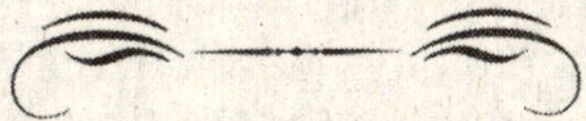

Writing may be a solitary endeavor, but it's never done without the support of others. Thank you to my editors Katie Gowrie and Tina James for the opportunity to participate in the Colorado K-9 Unit. Thank you to the other ladies of the continuity—Laura Scott, Sharon Dunn, Jodie Bailey, Sharee Stover, Jessica R. Patch, Maggie K. Black, Valerie Hansen, Lynette Eason and Lenora Worth—for all the brainstorming and encouragement. Thank you to my husband and son for feeding me and making sure I have everything I need while in my writing cave. And a big thank-you to author Leah Vale for reading each word and cheering me on.

ONE

K-9 Officer Maren Anderson battled the fatigue she'd been facing since driving from Colorado Springs to the Barren Valley Clinic in Barren Valley, Colorado. Grief could do that to a person. She'd been exhausted ever since she'd received the call a few months ago that her sister was dead. A pang pulled at her heart, threatening to derail her attention, but she needed to focus. Her partner, a Doberman pinscher named Haven, shifted closer to the chair Maren sat in across from the clinic director.

Sitting on the opposite side of the mahogany desk, the older woman with dark eyes and light blond hair cropped at her chin steepled her hands. The nameplate in gold lettering facing Maren read Dr. Victoria Newton.

Maren and Haven had come here following up on a lead about a discredited OB/GYN who'd once worked at this small practice in the sleepy mountain town. Maren hoped to find out more but didn't anticipate success.

The organized illegal adoption ring that she and her team were tracking had, so far, managed to stay one step ahead of law enforcement. Still, maybe today's interview could get her new information.

"Dr. Newton, do you believe that stolen babies are being sold illegally in the state of Colorado?" She was curious what the doctor knew about the subject.

Her K-9 seemed to lean forward with her, as if Haven also

had an interest in what the woman would say. All sleek lines with a red-and-brown coat, the dog wore a black vest with the words *K-9 Unit*. Haven was three years old and cross-trained in drug detection and suspect apprehension. And for good measure, protection.

Maren placed a calming hand on the dog's head, though inside, she was far from feeling calm. June sunshine streamed in through the window overlooking the main street, but a chill chased down her spine.

For months, the Colorado K-9 Unit had been searching for Mia Andrews, the missing, pregnant nineteen-year-old granddaughter of the task force's wealthy benefactor, Dodger Andrews. In the course of the search, three deceased young women were discovered in various parts of the state, each showing signs of having recently given birth. It was the discovery that someone was targeting vulnerable young pregnant women in that area that had that led to the task force being formed, comprising K-9 officers from around the Denver area.

They couldn't help but fear that Mia Andrews might be the next victim of a dangerous baby smuggling ring that was killing young moms and stealing their babies. Racing against time, the task force hoped to rescue Mia before her due date in October.

"You want to know if it's feasible that an operation like this exists?" Victoria gave a slow nod. "Not only possible, but probable. I've heard rumors that there is a black market rife with this sort of underhanded and often violent practice. Unfortunately, there are also some very unscrupulous doctors who will do anything for the large sums of cash being offered."

Maren sucked in a breath and slowly exhaled before asking, "Do you believe Dr. Derek Rolls could be involved?"

Victoria made a face. "Dr. Rolls lost his license two years ago and was booted from this clinic. And he left town as far as I've heard. He was involved in insurance fraud as well as being accused of writing prescriptions for various medications for nonpatients for a very high fee."

That aligned with the information they had gathered. The task force had been looking into any medical professionals who'd lost their licenses in the past five years. "Could he still be practicing medicine somewhere?"

"If he is, it's under a false identity or in some back room somewhere," Victoria said. "No reputable medical practice would touch him with a ten-foot pole."

"Do you happen to have a recent picture of Dr. Rolls?" Maren thought of the couple who had been spotted in a fancy SUV outside of a free clinic in Denver last month. The photo of Dr. Rolls that the task force had been able to dig up was from many years ago, when he was much younger.

A man and woman had seemed to be watching the obstetrician's office, leading the team to wonder if the occupants of the vehicle were scouring for vulnerable pregnant teens and young women with the intent to kidnap them and hold them until their delivery. The theory was the kidnappers would kill the women and sell their babies to unsuspecting adoptive couples who likely thought the high fees were mostly for prenatal care and the deliveries.

"No picture that I know of," the clinic director said. "I came on board after Dr. Rolls. I only know him by reputation." She reached forward to press a button on the desk phone. "Fran, can you come in here, please."

Moments later, the door opened and Fran, the clinic's receptionist, walked in. Maren put Fran in her mid- to late sixties and a throwback to the days of hippies and flower power, a fashion trend that had resurfaced of late. The woman had shaved the bottom half of her head, leaving a floppy top to be clipped in a colorful barrette. She had cat-eye-shaped eyeglasses in bright red and a silver nose ring as well as gauges in her ears. She wore a flowing top with wide-legged pants in a geometric pattern that made Maren's eyes hurt. She'd take her staid black pants, navy blazer and white blouse over bold colors any day.

"Is there a problem?" Fran asked, her blue gaze flicking to Maren and dropping to Haven, who stared back at her. Fran took a step back.

Haven could be intimidating even when not trying.

"You were here when Dr. Rolls was on staff, correct?" Victoria asked, drawing Fran's attention.

"I was." The derision in Fran's tone made it very clear she hadn't liked the doctor. "Good riddance, if you ask me."

"Do you have a photo?"

Fran shook her head. "He was very peculiar about having his picture taken."

"Can you give me a description of Dr. Rolls?" Maren held her breath, waiting to see if the description matched the man who had been seen outside the free clinic.

Fran's brow wrinkled. "He was tall, muscular. He had thinning reddish hair that he never seemed to comb, with a full beard, and he wore the strangest-looking silver eyeglasses." Fran touched her own glasses, adjusting them on her straight nose. "I don't think he needed corrective lenses, but he wore them anyway."

Maren nearly gasped aloud. It fit the description of their suspect. And the man had lost his medical license in the right time frame. There was a strong possibility that Dr. Rolls, the former OB/GYN of Barren Valley Clinic, was a part of the baby smuggling ring terrorizing the state of Colorado. Maren lifted up a prayer of hope that linking Dr. Rolls to the baby smugglers would help bring down the criminals and allow the team to rescue Mia.

"Do you know where he went after he left here?" Maren asked.

Fran shook her head. "No. I felt bad for his wife, though. She seemed nice enough."

Married? Could she be the woman they'd seen with him? "Do you remember her name or what she looks like?"

Fran scrunched up her nose. "No, to the name. Mousy-looking. I only met her once and briefly at that."

Blowing out a frustrated breath, Maren stood to hand Fran and Victoria her business card with the task force's main number on it. "If you think of anything that might be helpful or hear from Dr. Rolls, please let us know."

Victoria walked around her desk and escorted Maren and Haven to the lobby.

Maren noted another glass door entrance out the back of the building and spotted a patch of grass, a mature tree and a picnic table in the shade, no doubt for the staff to enjoy during their lunch breaks.

"I hope you find whoever's stealing and selling babies and make them stop," Victoria said. "It's hard enough for teenagers and young women lacking family support to get the medical care they need without them having to worry about being preyed upon by the doctors who are supposed to be caring for them."

Maren felt a pang at the thought of her own twin not having had the support she needed, which had most likely led to her death. Regret at having drifted apart from her sister lay heavy on Maren's shoulders.

"From your lips to God's ears." She shook the doctor's hand and then exited through the double glass doors at the front of the clinic.

She murmured a prayer for God to guide her as she hurried to her personal vehicle, a Ford Bronco with a specialized compartment for Haven. Once Haven was settled, Maren slipped into the driver's seat and fitted the key in the ignition.

However, she wasn't eager to return to her empty home.

Ever since joining the task force, the fact that she had no social life outside of work had become abundantly clear. But dating, romance and all the messiness that came with it wasn't something she longed to participate in. How could she risk any more heartache? Losing the last of her family was more than enough.

She was about to start the engine when her gaze landed on a woman walking through the parking lot toward the clinic.

No, it can't be!

Through the front windshield Maren stared at the woman in an army green jacket and black baggy pants hurrying toward the front doors.

Leaning forward in the driver's seat, she watched the woman, taking in the details.

Same long, light brown hair, same build and height.

Breathing turning shallow, she blinked hard to dispel the image of her twin sister, walking through the parking lot in front of her.

Because Opal was dead.

The stab of grief, as fresh as it had been three months ago when she'd learned of her sister's death, seared through Maren.

The Colorado Springs Police Department had determined that Opal Anderson had drowned. Her clothing and identification had been discovered beside the Arkansas River, a tributary of the Mississippi running through Colorado and known for its white water rafting. A river unsafe for swimming because of the strong currents and rocky bottom. Especially at night.

A witness had come forward claiming Opal had been high on drugs when she'd gone into the water. And never came back out. Her body had not been recovered.

Maren rubbed her eyes. She needed rest if she was seeing her dead sister alive and walking toward the clinic.

The woman paused and looked over her shoulder as if sensing she was being watched.

Maren gasped, the sound bouncing through the vehicle.

Her own face had just stared back at her.

Opal. Her twin was alive.

The woman disappeared inside the clinic.

Adrenaline fueling her actions, Maren popped open the driver's-side door and hopped out while depressing the button on her key fob that would release the hatch on the canine compartment door. Haven jumped out and stood waiting for a command.

Quickly leashing up her partner again, Maren hustled back toward the building. Her head buzzed with questions and her heart hammered against her ribs beneath the green Kevlar vest, which she always wore when working, hidden by her blouse and blazer. The June heat made her sweat, yet cold seeped into her bones.

A shiver of dread raced along her limbs.

This can't be happening.

Yet…as twins, Maren and Opal had often shared a strange sensory connection. A connection that had Maren questioning from the beginning if her sister was truly dead. After having searched the riverbank for miles, trying to find any sign of Opal but coming up empty, she was sure she'd have physically felt the loss of her twin.

As she approached the clinic door with Haven at her side, an uneasy feeling shifted through her, causing the hairs at her nape to lift with alarm. As she reached for the door handle, Haven spun, faced the street and let out a series of frantic barks.

Having worked with Haven for over two years, Maren knew the tone of her partner's bark.

Haven was alerting to danger.

But from where? And who?

Before Maren could formulate an action plan, gunfire rang out. Bullets pelted the building around her, coming within inches of slamming into her or Haven. The clinic doors exploded in a shower of glass. Terrified screams echoed from within.

Acting quickly, Maren crouched and reined in Haven's leash.

She hustled them both toward the nearest parked car to use as cover as more bullets peppered the front of the clinic and sidewalk.

Using the wheel well of a luxury vehicle parked at the curb in front of the building, and keeping Haven out of the line of fire, Maren reached for her cell phone. She called for backup and asked the dispatcher to alert her task force boss, FBI Special Agent Emmett Dane, that she was in trouble at the Barren Valley Clinic location. She was trapped and under fire.

Drawing her weapon, she debated returning fire. She wasn't sure where the shots were coming from.

Why was someone shooting? Was she the target? Did this have to do with the illegal baby adoption ring? Or was she just in the wrong place and the wrong time? Could the onslaught of firepower be aimed at the clinic itself?

Aggravation chomped through her veins. She hadn't been able to catch the woman who looked like her twin, maybe even *was* her twin, before she'd entered the clinic. Could she have actually been her sister? Was she the shooter's target?

Or was her mind so fatigued that she'd imagined the resemblance?

Crouched behind the car for cover, she prayed backup arrived soon and braced herself for the shooter to strike again.

DEA Agent Colt Dawson and his K-9 partner, a German shorthaired pointer named Rusk, raced toward the woman, who was an exact replica of the suspect he'd been trailing. She and her dog were hunkered down behind a parked sedan. The woman had an arm around the Doberman, but he could also see she'd drawn a weapon.

Who was she? Some sort of law enforcement, obviously, if the vest on her K-9 was real. But which agency and why was she here? The woman he was trailing, Opal Anderson, definitely wasn't law enforcement.

But he'd learned the hard way that people could be deceptive and sometimes the truth was difficult to discern. He'd made the mistake of trusting the wrong woman once before, but never again.

Confusion warred within his brain now as he assessed the situation. He'd been following the associate of the drug kingpin known as Shadow, hoping she'd lead him to the man responsible for so many illegal drug overdoses in the state of Colorado.

He had a personal interest in stopping the flow. After his own cousin OD'd, he'd spent most of his professional life in law enforcement on a quest to bring an end to the poison.

A tip from one of the DEA's informants had alleged that the supposedly dead Opal Anderson was actually alive and hiding out in Barren Valley, Colorado, and would be able to give a location for Shadow. Could she identify the criminal?

Colt was counting on it.

Needing to follow the lead, Colt had hightailed it from Colorado Springs, where he'd been pounding the pavement trying to shake loose information on Shadow, to the flea-bitten motel on the edge of Barren Valley's main drag.

For two days, he'd staked out the motel, waiting for some sign of the woman. He'd just about given up, thinking the break he'd been hoping for was turning into a dead end, when this morning, Opal Anderson had emerged from one of the rooms and caught the bus into town.

Colt had trailed her, and when the woman had disembarked at the stop near the clinic and approached the building, he'd parked and planned to follow her inside. He'd intended to corner her with the hope of flipping her to help them find Shadow.

He'd been momentarily distracted when he'd seen the other woman climb out of a brown-and-black Bronco.

The woman looked eerily like Opal Anderson. Only where Opal was gaunt, with hollowed-out cheeks and stringy hair, this officer looked healthy and agile as she and her K-9 partner had hurried after Opal.

But then, the world had turned to chaos seconds after Opal entered the clinic. The unknown woman was being shot at.

Keeping Rusk at his heels, Colt aimed his own firearm to where the shots had originated. A brick, four-story building across the street from the clinic.

He needed to find out what was happening.

The sound of footsteps running toward Maren had her tensing. Still crouched, she pivoted on the balls of her feet with her sidearm gripped now in both hands. Was the shooter coming for her?

Her gaze snagged on the identifying windbreaker. A mix of relief and irritation swept through her as a chestnut-haired man with a close-cropped beard and mustache raced to her side with a gun at the ready. Close at his heels was a brown-and-white German shorthaired pointer. Haven's ears twitched, the only sign she was aware of the other dog.

If not for the emblem of the drug enforcement agency on the breast pocket of his jacket, Maren would have defended herself. Why was the DEA here?

She had no great love for the federal agency that hadn't been able to stop the influx of drugs coming into the state. If the DEA had done a better job, maybe Opal wouldn't have been able to so easily get a hold of the various drugs that she used to numb herself.

Maren had half a mind to break cover and run to the clinic, but she knew her boss would want her to wait for backup. Plus, with Haven in the line of fire, she couldn't risk her dog's safety. Haven was her constant companion, the one who helped her get through the dark days of overwhelming grief after receiving the news of her twin sister's death.

But now, did she dare hope? No. It would hurt too much if

she were wrong. And it would hurt if she was right, because that would mean her sister had faked her death and deliberately allowed Maren to suffer.

Meeting the green eyes of the DEA agent grounded Maren's thoughts to the moment.

"Who are you? Why are you here?" she demanded to know of the agent crouched beside her, who popped up to returned fire toward the building across the street. "Did dispatch send you?"

"I could ask you the same thing," he said in a terse voice as he ducked back down to avoid another volley of bullets raging from the brick building. "What branch of law enforcement are you?"

Tucking her chin, Maren exclaimed, "How do you know—"

He arched an eyebrow, his gaze going to Haven and her police vest.

Grunting, she said, "Colorado Springs PD. On loan to the Colorado K-9 Unit task force and deputized as a federal agent." She added that last bit to make it clear they were equals as the drug enforcement agency also fell under federal jurisdiction. "You are…?"

"Agent Colt Dawson," he said and tapped his chest where the letters proclaimed which agency he was with.

"You didn't answer my question." She frowned. "Why are you here?"

"Neither did you," he said. "Are you in league with Opal Anderson?"

Maren's lungs squeezed tight at the mention of her sister's name. Then outrage infused her brain. "In league with? What are you talking about?"

"If you're helping her," Colt said between gritted teeth, "I will make sure you go down."

Maren curled her lip at the man. "I'm here on an assignment. Why are you looking for Opal?"

"Why are you?"

"I'm not," Maren ground out. The agent had to be mistaken.

That wasn't Opal. It couldn't be. It was some weird coincidence that the woman looked like her twin. After all, she'd only caught a quick glimpse of the woman before the clinic was shot up. And her grief over her sister had her seeing Opal everywhere. "I don't know who that woman was who walked into the clinic. But I'm going to find out."

She moved to stand, but a firm hand on her shoulder kept her in place.

"First, we have to find out who's using the clinic as a shooting gallery," he said. "And if you're the intended target."

Her stomach twisted. Why would someone want her dead? She had to find out if the woman was her sister or not. And was she in danger, too? Why was the DEA after her?

Another barrage of gunfire pinged off the car and had Maren ducking, while Colt popped up to shoot back at the brick building across the street. The shrill sound of sirens punctuated the air, announcing the arrival of backup.

TWO

The gunfire ceased as the Barren Valley County Sheriff's Department descended on scene outside the clinic. Colt stood and held out his hand for the woman beside him.

She swatted away his offered limb and cautiously rose, keeping her gaze on the brick building across the street.

"There!" Maren pointed to a tall figure emerging from the side of the building where the shots had originated. The person was dressed all in black with a baseball cap pulled low over their head, shielding their face.

Jolted into action, he and Rusk gave chase, aware of Maren and her Doberman hot on their heels.

"Halt, Police!" Colt yelled.

The suspect swung an automatic rifle in their direction and sprayed the sidewalk with bullets.

Colt scooped Rusk up with one arm, twisted away from the shooter to shield Maren and her dog, who dove to the side between two cars.

The pounding of feet had his gaze jerking back in time to see the shooter running away and rounding the corner. He clenched his jaw with frustration.

Focusing back on the officer, he studied her face. High cheek bones, soft blue eyes and honey brown hair highlighted with golden streaks. She wore dark pants, a navy blazer and a white blouse. He recognized the bulk of a bulletproof vest beneath the top. "Are you hurt?"

"No," she said, though there was a definite tremor to her voice. She stood. "You?"

He shook his head as his gaze snagged on a small cross necklace around her neck glinting in the sunlight. Apparently, the simple symbol of her faith was the only jewelry she wore. Not that he was looking at her ring finger.

But still, he noted the lack of a wedding band.

Her dog sat at her side, dark eyes watching him and Rusk. To Rusk's credit, the pointer, usually high-strung and raring to go, remained calm though poised to take off at any second.

"Look, I'm sorry if I offended you earlier," Colt said. "Help me understand what's happening here. You're the spitting image of the woman who just entered the clinic."

Ignoring him, the K-9 officer and her partner hurried back the way they'd come and went straight to the sheriff, a big man wearing a brown uniform and cowboy hat. Colt and Rusk trailed after them but kept a distance so she could give the sheriff her account of what happened. The sheriff sent deputies into the building across the street.

Colt doubted they would find the perpetrator. But hopefully the sniper would have left behind brass to give them a clue.

The sheriff, whose name tag read Wallen, and the K-9 officer turned toward him as he and Rusk halted at the woman's side.

"Sheriff Wallen." Colt held out his hand. "DEA. Colt Dawson."

The sheriff's handshake was firm. "Maren here was telling me you showed up seconds after the shots were fired."

"Yes, sir. I was down the street surveilling a suspect," Colt said.

Maren. He liked that name. Strong. Stubborn. Like the woman who bore the name.

"What's the DEA's involvement here?" Maren demanded to know.

Arching an eyebrow, he said, "I received a tip-off that an associate of a drug kingpin who I'm trying to bring down was lying low in this fair town."

"I wasn't informed of your presence," Wallen huffed.

"It was a last-minute operation," Colt explained. Though he'd had time to reach out to the local law enforcement, he wasn't sure whom to trust. Colt had been on the case tracking Shadow for nearly a year, and the suspect, yet to be identified, always seemed to be one step ahead of the authorities. Because he had moles within the justice system?

"You mentioned my sister by name," Maren said. "What makes you think my twin is still alive?"

Surprise washed through him. Sisters. Twins. That explained the resemblance. "You saw her with your own eyes. Opal Anderson is not dead despite reports saying otherwise. She's the girlfriend of an associate of one of the DEA's most wanted criminals."

Maren's brow wrinkled as she digested this information. Colt's gaze dropped to her bow-shaped mouth, tracing her full lips. Then he jerked his gaze up and met her blue eyes.

There was no way he was going to let a pretty face and an interesting personality infiltrate the barriers he'd erected around his heart. The last time he'd dropped his defenses, he'd paid the price.

Disconcerted by the unwelcome direction of his thoughts, he turned to the sheriff. "If you need anything else from me, give me a call." He handed the sheriff one of his business cards. "I've a job to do. I need to find my suspect."

Colt and Rusk strode away while he ticked off the seconds in his head. How long would it take for Officer Maren Anderson to catch up?

Seething, Maren watched the arrogant and irritating DEA agent heading for the clinic door, which now was just a metal frame with broken glass littering the sidewalk. The man stopped, patted his chest and the shorthaired pointer jumped into his arms.

If the agent thought he was going into the clinic without her, he was horribly mistaken.

"Sheriff, do you mind?" She gestured toward the clinic, the urgency and need to discover the truth returning. "I have to find out if Opal is alive. I need to see her."

Empathy darkened his gaze. "Not at all. I know where to find you if I need you."

"Come, Haven, we have a job to do."

As she approached the door, from inside the clinic lobby, the DEA agent called out, "Watch your step. The glass is tricky."

Making a face at his retreating back, she called back, "I'm aware."

No way would she admit that she'd been distracted by her annoyance and might have charged into the building with Haven at her side without considering the danger to her dog's paws until it was too late.

She needed to do better. Be better.

Taking a breath to prepare, she picked Haven up and carried her across the broken glass. With each step, Maren tried to ignore the fact that the handsome and irritating agent had been looking out for her partner. She didn't need him or any man looking out for her or Haven. They were doing just fine on their own.

Her heart thudded within her chest at the possibility of finding her presumed dead sister inside this clinic. If it even was Opal, was she okay?

Colt stepped inside the clinic that appeared empty. No one manned the reception desk, no patients sat in the waiting area. Most likely everyone had taken care and found safe places to lie low, fearing the gunman would come inside. Empathy spread through his chest. His gaze went to the back door of the clinic, which stood open. Had someone fled out the back? Had Opal?

Maren, carrying her Doberman, entered the lobby. He was impressed by her strength since he had no doubt that dog was heavy.

When it was safe, she set the dog down and they moved to stand beside him.

"Everyone must be hiding," she said and turned to walk down the hallway leading to empty exam rooms and offices.

He had to admit to himself, as they fell into step, that he was intrigued by the K-9 officer and her connection to the suspect. Sisters. No, twins.

Why hadn't he known there was a sibling? A twin, no less. A twin who was a cop.

He'd been too focused on finding Shadow to do a deep dive on Opal, even when he'd arrested her for drug possession on numerous occasions.

He wouldn't admit, however, that he'd been upset to see Maren in danger. Not her specifically, he told himself. Anyone in danger. It scratched at an old scar. Reminded him of the one life he hadn't been able to save.

They found a group of staff and patients huddled behind an overturned round table in the break room.

"It's safe," he said, using a gentle tone. "The shooter is gone."

Several pregnant women were helped to their feet by nurses and doctors.

"What happened?" A formidable woman strode forward.

"Dr. Newton," Maren said. "We're not sure why someone was shooting at the clinic."

Colt gave the officer a sidelong glance. "Or who the intended target was. It could have been Opal, but she'd already entered the building by the time the shooting started."

The displeased glare Maren shot at him made him press his lips together to keep from allowing a snarky remark to pass.

Maren obviously didn't want to think of herself as being the target. But what other explanation could there be for the shooting?

"Excuse me, Doctor, we're looking for a woman who looks like her—" He pointed a thumb at Maren. "Do you know where she is?"

The doctor shook her head. "Fran?"

An older woman with trendy glasses and the sides of her dark, salted hair shaved, stepped forward and stared at Maren. "Weren't you here earlier?"

"I was," Maren confirmed.

She was?

Curiosity piqued, Colt wanted to know what had brought the K-9 officer to the clinic. It hadn't been pure coincidence that Maren and her sister were at the same place.

More questions bubbled in his mind. Was Maren at the clinic on police business as she'd claimed? Or was it more personal? Was she expecting? Just a checkup?

Or to meet her sister?

Suspicion reared. Was the officer telling him the truth about not knowing her twin was alive?

Shaking her head, Fran said, "Can't say that I've seen anyone else who looks like you."

Maren huffed out a breath. "We saw her enter the clinic just before the shooting."

"I was getting coffee when I heard the gunfire," Fran said with a shrug.

"Several people ran out the back door," a nurse said in passing, confirming Colt's earlier thought.

Frustrated that he'd missed his opportunity to corner Opal, Colt asked, "Can you check to see if you have any no-show appointments for the past half hour."

Fran nodded and they followed her back to the reception desk. She checked her records. "As a matter of fact," the receptionist said, "we have one. Anna Parker didn't show. Or at least, she didn't get checked in before the shooting started."

Anna Parker. Must be the phony name Opal had given when she'd made the appointment.

Maren's hands fisted on the reception counter. "What was she going to be seen for?"

Fran's eyebrows hitched upward. The overhead light reflected off the silver-studded piercing in her left brow. "I can't divulge that information. HIPAA and all that."

Colt knew that without a warrant they wouldn't obtain information on Anna Parker. But he could have a warrant within hours. If it meant bringing down Shadow, he would do whatever it took.

Though his goal of flipping his suspect was going to be delayed, Colt trusted that God would see justice done. But at least he was one step closer by learning the alias his suspect was going by. When he ran Anna Parker through the databases, what would surface? And would the information lead him to Shadow?

Without another word, Maren headed for the lobby.

Clicking his tongue for Rusk to follow, they jogged to keep up, stopping at the edge of the scattered, broken glass. Going any farther would be dangerous for the canines.

"What are you really doing here?" he asked Maren.

She frowned as she picked up her dog. The Doberman looked heavy in her arms. "It's a need-to-know matter, and you don't need to know."

Reining in his frustration, he patted his chest. Rusk sprang up and he easily wrapped him in his arms.

Maren walked out of the building.

Colt stayed close. "Look, we're both working toward justice. Whatever it is you're investigating has made you a target."

"We don't know that for sure." Her eyes narrowed, the shade of blue deepening. "I have people who will watch my back."

As they moved away from the clinic toward the parking lot, he asked, "And where are they?"

Irritation marched across her face. The woman was so easy to read.

She set the dog down. Her gaze swept the parking lot. "This was supposed to be a simple interview," she said softly. "I didn't think I would require—"

Taking pity on her, he gentled his tone. "Look, let's just work together while we're here. I told you why I'm at this clinic. The least you can do is quid pro quo."

Maren heaved a sigh. "I can tell you that I'm investigating an illegal adoption scheme where three young mothers have been murdered and a pregnant teenager is missing. One of the suspects we believe to be involved may have worked at the clinic, which I confirmed."

Shock reverberated through him. A violent baby smuggling ring? Who would do such a thing? Disgust filled his chest. He'd always considered the drug trade a deplorable industry, but the illegal buying and selling of babies…murder…?

No wonder someone was trying to keep the officer from her quest. His respect for Maren ratcheted up. He decided, then and there, that sticking close to the K-9 officer was the right thing to do, because she needed somebody watching her back here and now. She'd mentioned she had backup but they weren't on scene at the moment.

Part of him looked forward to sparring with the pretty officer.

Not good, Dawson.

The last thing he needed was to let emotions of any sort cloud his judgment. He'd faltered on that score before, receiving a deep, scalding wound that had yet to heal. When it came to women, he didn't seem to have any common sense. Best to just bolster his barriers so they couldn't be breached.

He would keep things professional between them. He couldn't

forget his own agenda. Sticking close to Maren would lead him to Opal and to his ultimate goal of taking down Shadow.

He didn't want to think about Maren and her twin getting caught in the cross fire.

THREE

Maren stomped toward her Bronco parked in the lot of the clinic with Haven at her side. Her blood boiled. This whole situation had turned into a complication that was equally upsetting and painful.

Her sister.

Alive?

Did she dare hope?

Though she was satisfied she'd been able to confirm Dr. Derek Rolls's last-known place of employment, seeing a woman who looked like her sister—her heart bumped—who could have been her sister—had sent her into a tailspin.

And now to learn this DEA agent was hunting Opal like she was a criminal?

Aware of Colt and his dog, a beautiful German shorthaired pointer he called Rusk, trailing behind them, she stopped short of her car and turned to face them.

Haven, apparently mistaking Maren's upset for a sign of danger, moved to stand in front of her as if guarding her from an oncoming threat.

"Friend," she murmured, letting the dog know to stand down. Haven sat but stayed in front of her.

Colt stopped, with his dog at his heels. The pointer sat with his tongue lolling to the side.

"Why are you following me?" she demanded to know.

Arching an eyebrow, he said, "I'm not letting you out of my sight."

His matter-of-fact tone grated on her nerves.

"That's not necessary," she said. "The shooter is long gone. We don't even know why he was shooting at the clinic."

"I think we do know why," Colt said. "You're digging into a very dangerous organization."

She hated to admit the real possibility that someone connected to the illegal adoption scheme was targeting her. But how anyone could have known she was coming here was a mystery. She'd only learned of the lead last night from Eva Gomez, tech analyst for the task force, and then driven to the clinic this morning. "What do you know about it?"

"Not as much as I would like," he said. "Let me help you."

Her defenses rose. Did he think she couldn't handle her job? Who was he to judge her? "I have a whole task force helping," she said. "What could you do?"

"We both know your sister's not dead," he said. "I found her once. I can find her again."

A lancing pain struck her to the core. Why would Opal make her suffer? "We know no such thing. Just because that woman—" Even as the words left her mouth, she knew they were a lie. It had been Opal. But now she was in the wind, once again lost to Maren. But not dead. She took a shuddering breath. The exhaustion she'd been fighting returned. "Why were you following Opal?"

Colt's eyebrows twitched. "You do believe she was your sister."

Blowing out a breath, she admitted, "For now, I will allow there's a good possibility that Opal is alive."

The thought conjured up a ton of questions, alongside a tsunami of hurt. If her sister was alive, why would she make Maren go through the ordeal of believing she was dead? Especially after the way they'd lost their parents to a car crash when they were eighteen. And then their uncle who'd taken them in had had a heart attack. Her twin was the only family she had left. Maren hoped that if she were open and helpful regarding Opal, then maybe the DEA would give her more information on her sister's case.

Wariness evident in his eyes, Colt asked, "What made you change your mind?"

She debated how much to say. She didn't know this man. And she wasn't sure she could trust him. But he was her best chance of reuniting with her twin.

If Opal was involved somehow with this drug kingpin, then Maren needed to protect her. "I don't know if you understand the bond that twins share, but Opal and I have always been aware when the other was in trouble or hurt."

Memories surfaced, taking her back to when they were young. "When we were eight, I fell from the balance beam at gymnastics camp and broke my arm. Opal, who had been at band camp that summer, knew I was hurt. She wouldn't relent until the camp counselors let her call our parents, who told her what had happened. I had to leave camp early and Opal insisted on coming home early, too." Shaking her head at her sister's tenacity, she continued, "Then in our late teens, she'd slipped on ice and fractured her tailbone. I felt the pain, even though I was miles away at a gymnastics competition."

"You two were close," he said. "But it sounds like you had different interests."

"We did. She was more artsy and sensitive while I couldn't sit still." Resolved, she admitted, "When I was told Opal was dead, I didn't feel it." She thumped her chest. "Even though everyone around me told me to let her go. That she was gone, lost to the river…deep down, I couldn't accept it."

"I believe you," he said. "My sister has twin daughters. They're about to turn six and seem to be able to communicate with each other without words. I've no doubt you sensed that your sister was alive. Despite everything and everyone telling you otherwise."

Not sure how to digest his support, she said, "None of that negates the fact that your agency has failed to bring down this opioid monster that you think Opal can identify."

"Touché," he says. "I apologize on behalf of the Drug Enforcement Agency. It's been a long and arduous investigation with many moving pieces. My boss and I both agree that the man known as Shadow has connections within various law enforcement agencies that has kept him protected."

She hated to think there was a traitor among those who served their communities. But she knew it happened. No one was infallible. People were vulnerable to greed and blackmail. Could there be a mole somewhere along the line in law enforcement keeping the adoption racket protected, too?

Even those who had faith could be led down dark roads. Just like Opal. The grief her sister carried had led her to a destructive path.

"I need to check in with my boss," Maren told Colt as she shook off the memories. "If he gives me the okay, then we can compare notes and see what we can come up with to help both of our investigations."

Colt inclined his head in agreement.

Maren popped open the special K-9 compartment in the back and clicked into her cheek. Haven immediately turned and jumped inside.

"I'm parked over there," he said, indicating a small compact truck with a camper shell over the bed.

Eyeing the older vehicle, she said, "Not what I would have expected."

"Don't let the old girl fool you. It's fully equipped with a specialized air-conditioned unit for Rusk in the back camper."

Not wanting to admit she was impressed, she nodded. "Give me your number. I'll let you know what my boss says."

He rattled off his number and she entered it into her cell phone, storing it under his name. Then she climbed into the cab of her Bronco, started the engine and blasted the AC.

She watched as Colt and Rusk hurried across the street to his unassuming yet fancy rig. The back hatch popped open, and Rusk jumped inside. Colt closed the tailgate, concealing the dog. He gave Maren a wave before he slipped into the driver's seat.

She called her boss in the task force unit, Emmett Dane.

"Maren, I trust you're calling with an update," Emmett said by way of greeting.

"Yes, sir. I've confirmed that Dr. Derek Rolls once worked at the OB clinic here in Barren Valley. The description given by one of the employees matches that of the man seen at the free clinic in Denver."

"Good. That's all good," Emmett said. "But I want to know how you are. A shooting? Explain to me what happened."

She told him the situation, including spotting her supposedly dead twin sister.

"You've had a rough morning," he said. "I can send someone your way as backup. I would have sooner but everyone's out working various angles on the case."

For months the task force members had been going to clinics and asking after suspicious incidents. And warning doctors and staff about the danger to young moms in the area. Everyone promised to keep vigilant and to ask their patients to as well.

Her gaze went to the brown truck. "About that," she said. "DEA Agent Colt Dawson would like to be read in on our investigation. We want to see if somehow his search for a drug kingpin and our search for this illegal adoption ring intersect." Could the two investigations share the same mole within law enforcement?

Guilt pricked at her for not mentioning their shared goal of finding her sister.

"I would imagine that you and Agent Dawson are both eager to locate Opal."

Maren winced. That was why Emmett was the boss. Perceptive and highly intelligent. Nothing got by him. "Yes, sir. But I promise I won't lose sight of our mission."

"Maren, you don't have to sell me on this," Emmett said. "I believe in you. Otherwise, I wouldn't have asked for you to join the task force. I'll reach out to the DEA. In the meantime, you have my permission to read Agent Dawson in on our investigation. If you two can work together, then I don't have to reallocate resources."

Pleasure at hearing that her boss had confidence in her made her expel a pent-up breath. "Thank you. I will keep you abreast of any information that will pertain to our investigation."

"I'm sure you will," Emmett replied. "Find this woman. Find out if she *is* your sister. Maybe she'll know something helpful. If nothing else, it will give you closure one way or another."

Closure.

Something she hadn't had when their parents were killed, nor when her sister supposedly drowned.

"I appreciate it, sir."

Emmett signed off and Maren sat for a moment, taking deep, calming breaths to ease the knotting of anxiety in her stomach.

When she was ready, she dialed Agent Dawson's number. He picked up on the first ring.

"Officer Anderson."

She sighed. "Call me Maren. I talked to my boss. He said to read you in. He's calling your boss now."

"Wonderful," Colt said.

She could hear the smile in his voice. It did funny things to her insides.

Putting steel into her own voice, she said, "We both have a common goal. To find Opal. Or at least the woman we think is Opal. By joining forces, maybe we can discover something that will help us solve both of our cases."

"Sounds like a good plan."

"What do you think my sister was doing at the clinic?" Maren asked, her brain filing through different scenarios. "I hate to think she is working for the illegal adoption ring."

Colt's voice softened. "I get the feeling you don't want to think she might be pregnant."

Maren's heart thumped. Sweat broke out along the nape of her neck. Opal pregnant? Wouldn't Maren have felt that sort of change in her sister? Maybe the twin connection that she'd always put so much stock in was just an illusion. Something she and Opal had made up. Yet, the many instances of their uncanny link belied that thought. Maybe it was Opal's drug use. "Before my sister's supposed drowning, she went off the grid. I'd been unable to find her."

"So really, you have no idea who she's been associating with," Colt's voice filled the cab. "My informant vows she's the girlfriend of one of Shadow's top lieutenants."

Sadness mixed with regret made her wince. So much lost time with Opal. If only they'd remained in touch, things would be so different. She'd have known who Opal was involved with.

Staring at the truck where Colt sat, she asked, "You trust this informant?"

"No way," Colt scoffed. "He's a drug addict. But most of his intel thus far has been spot-on. I can't say for sure that he's not playing both sides, feeding the DEA information and then feeding Shadow information. He could be the leak that keeps Shadow from our grasp."

"That's a hard call," Maren said. "I want to see where my sister was staying."

"Okay, follow me," he said.

Maren followed the brown truck to the edge of town and

pulled into the parking lot of an old, run-down, two-story motel that probably should have been condemned years ago.

She parked beneath the shade of a tree and kept the engine running. Colt and his dog hurried to her car. He climbed in the passenger's side with his K-9 sitting on his lap.

He pointed. "She came out of room 210."

"Let's see if she's returned." Maren turned off the engine and reached for the door handle.

Colt stopped her with a hand on her arm. "We don't know who else is in that room."

Eyeing the peeling green paint curling around the brown doors, she said, "Have you seen anyone else going in and out?"

"I haven't," he said. "But that doesn't mean there might not be more people involved. I sat here for two days waiting for that door to open. And when it did, Opal stepped out."

Needing to know if Opal was there, she said, "We have to risk it. I need to do this." She took a beat before adding, "I should go alone."

"No way." He opened the passenger door and turned to look at her. "Let me lead. My investigation."

Not liking having someone else in charge, she frowned. She was stepping on his investigation, but it was her sister that might be in that room. Maybe all the more reason for her to allow him to take point. "Fine."

With their dogs at their heels, they made their way across the parking lot. The heat coming off thc pavement made them hurry to protect the paws of their canines.

They made their way up the staircase to the second floor and proceeded down the cement corridor and approached room 210.

The window shades were drawn closed. They couldn't see inside.

Colt rapped his knuckles on the door. Rusk stood at his side. His body tense as if he expected to protect his partner.

No response to Colt's knock.

"Housekeeping," Maren called out. Beside her, Haven shifted as if ready to lunge at the door.

Colt glanced over his shoulder at her. She wasn't sure how to take his raised eyebrows. Approval or reprimand?

She shrugged, unapologetic.

Still no answer or movement from inside the motel room.

Colt tried the brass doorknob. It easily turned in his hand. He unholstered his sidearm and pushed the door open.

Holding her firearm at the ready, Maren tapped his shoulder to let him know she was on his six. Her heart hammered against her ribs as they entered the room.

Neither dog alerted.

They were greeted by orange shag carpet, with one of the two queen beds mussed as if recently slept in, and the remnants of fast-food wrappers littering the desk and floor.

Colt cleared the bathroom.

He holstered his gun. "She apparently didn't come back."

"She might still show up." Maren couldn't help the hope in her voice.

He gave her a sympathetic look. "Do you really believe that?"

No, she didn't believe Opal would return. Not with dangerous drug dealers on her tail who wanted to keep her from possibly identifying the boss to the authorities. This was a dead end. "How long have you been following my sister?"

Maren couldn't believe how easily those words rolled off her tongue. Now that she'd basically accepted her sister was alive, the urge to see her and hug her was strong.

"Five days ago, my informant told me that someone who looks a lot like the supposedly dead Opal Anderson was hiding out in Barren Valley. Though this town is small, there are places here that someone could easily hide in."

"That doesn't explain how you identified her."

He grimaced. "I'm sorry to say, I've arrested your sister a few times in the past."

"That doesn't surprise me." Hurt and disappointment permeated her chest. Opal's drug use had started right after their parents' death and continued on. No matter how much Maren pleaded with her to go to rehab, Opal had refused. "Clearly, she never mentioned she had a twin."

"No, she did not. Nor did she mention her sister was in law enforcement. Maybe things would have gone differently for her if she had." Colt's gaze turned intense. "I sense there was estrangement between you two. Why?"

"She didn't like that I went into law enforcement." She remembered the arguments. The accusations. The guilt and blame. "Or that I wouldn't give up searching for our parents' killer."

His mouth dropped open, then snapped shut. "Your parents were killed?"

"Hit-and-run." Even talking about it brought up all the impotent rage that had fueled her to excel through the police academy. "No witnesses. No cameras in the area."

Colt frowned. "The driver was never caught?"

"No. Plus, we were eighteen at the time. Not exactly in a position to push the police to do more."

"And that's what drove you to pursue a career in law enforcement."

The empathy in his expression had her throat closing. "Unfortunately, Opal dealt with our parents' death by checking out and numbing herself with drugs."

Colt took her hand. "I am sorry for your loss."

She slipped her hand away because the contact made her feel uncomfortable and comforted at the same time.

She needed to stay grounded. Focus on the here and now. On what she could control. First order of business was finding Opal. "Tell me everything you know about Opal and her supposed death."

"Don't you have access to the police file?"

"I do," she said. "I've read it cover to cover. I know what it says. But I want to know what your take on the situation is."

Colt nodded. "On the night she was presumed to have died, Opal and a companion bought a two-ounce bag of fentanyl-laced opioids off a low-level drug dealer. Four hours later, a witness—" He paused, pulling his eyebrows together. "Vinnie Homer. He reported the drowning."

Pulse thrumming, Maren leaned forward, reciting the words she'd memorized. "The police report stated Opal had been high and had left her clothing and identification on the riverbank before wading into the Arkansas River. She went under and never came back up. The next morning her necklace was found downstream in a tangle of bushes." Tears pricked the back of Maren's eyes. "I gave her that necklace."

"I'm sure you could reclaim it," Colt said softly.

Something Maren had thought about over the past three months but had never acted on.

"I want to talk to your informant." Maren's breathing accelerated. "Do you think he helped my sister fake her death? And if so, why lead you here? Why fake her death at all?"

"All good questions," Colt said. "I can arrange for us to meet him." He picked up a pencil from the desk and sifted through the garbage can. "Maren, you should see this."

Moving to his side, she gave a little gasp. Deep in the wastebasket was an empty bottle of prenatal vitamins.

Could Opal be pregnant?

Anxiety twisted in her gut. "But we can't be sure those are hers."

"One way to find out." Colt reached into his pants pocket for a clear evidence bag and fished the bottle out of the trash can, then slipped the bottle into the bag. He stuffed the evidence into the pocket of his cargo pants. "I'll have our lab run fingerprints."

"Even if her prints are on the bottle, it doesn't mean more than that she was taking care of herself," Maren stated.

The sympathetic expression on his face had her turning away. She swallowed the emotions rearing up.

Her sister could very well be having a baby. It made sense now why she had gone to the clinic. The urgency to find Opal intensified.

After searching the motel room for anything that could tell them where Opal would go next and coming up with nothing, they left the motel and hurried back to their respective cars.

As she drove away from the motel, a barrage of bullets pelted her Bronco. The back tire blew with a loud bang and the SUV jolted. Heart hammering hard enough to pound metal, she lost control and swerved into a ditch on the four-lane highway. A blue panel van pulled up alongside her, the door slid open and a masked man jumped out.

Was it the same masked man in black who'd shot up the clinic?

Fearing she was about to die, she dove sideways into the passenger seat. Haven's frantic, aggressive barks echoed in her ears. Thankfully, she was locked securely in her compartment.

The mask man used the butt of his automatic rifle to break out the window. "You should have stayed dead. No one crosses Shadow and lives."

Having no time to process his words, she braced for another barrage of bullets, and lifted a prayer asking God to spare her life.

Gunfire rang out.

FOUR

Panic gripping him in a tight vise, Colt bolted from his truck, firing at the gunman standing beside Maren's car. Had the guy already put a bullet in Maren?

A wave of dread and nausea rolled over Colt.

The man spun and shot back at him. Colt dove to the side, rolled and came up on one knee, firing again at the gunman. The masked assailant screamed as a bullet lodged in his shoulder, and he practically fell back into the van.

The vehicle took off in a squeal of tires, taking the injured gunman with it.

Fearing for Maren, Colt lunged to his feet and ran to the Bronco, now lodged front-end first in the ditch on the side of the road. The second Colt watched the van race up behind Maren's vehicle, he'd known something bad was going down. Seeing her back tire blow had his heart jumping into his throat.

But then, when the van jerked to a stop and a masked man jumped out, he'd nearly crashed into the ditch as well. He'd managed to stop in time to fend off the attack. At least he hoped so.

He reached the driver's side of Maren's vehicle. His heart slammed into his throat. She was slumped over onto the passenger seat. Her dark hair created a curtain that concealed her face. There was no visible blood that he could see but the lack didn't mean she was unharmed. White powder from the steering wheel airbag floated in the air, landing on the glittering chunks of glass spewed all over Maren's back and the driver's seat.

From the back, Haven barked frantically and scratched at the partition between her compartment and the front seat.

"I know, I know," Colt reassured the dog as he reached in through the broken shards left in the windowsill and undid the door latch, pulling the door open.

He reached for Maren, praying he wasn't too late.

"Maren?" he said softly. His hands landed on her shoulders with a tremor running up his arms.

Please, Lord, please, don't let her be injured. Or worse.

Slowly, she turned her head. Her panicked gaze met his. Then relief filled her face.

"It's you," she breathed out and sat up. Glass from the broken window slid off her back.

Unable to help himself he gathered her into his arms, cupping her face in his hands. "Are you hurt?"

"I don't think so." For a moment, she was pliant in his arms, then she pulled back, forcing him to release her. "I need to let Haven out."

She reached for the key fob dangling from the ignition and popped open the side panel. Within seconds, the Doberman was crowding next to Colt in the open driver's-side doorframe and frantically licking her partner's face.

"Whoa, whoa," Maren said gently, fending off the dog. "I'm okay. Everybody back up."

Grabbing Haven's collar, Colt tugged the dog away from the SUV, allowing Maren space so she could climb out of the vehicle.

"You're sure you're not hurt?" He heard the concern in his voice but was helpless to stop it. Scenes like this brought back memories of his cousin's overdose and eventual death. Colt had been the one to find him and had done CPR, to no avail.

She tested her limbs and her neck before saying, "Everything seems to be in working order."

Relief that she appeared unharmed flooded his system.

Her gaze dropped to Haven, who now sat quietly at Colt's side. He still had a hold of the collar.

Maren's mouth twisted in a wry grimace. "She usually doesn't behave for anyone else but me."

"I think these are extenuating circumstances." He released his hold on the dog.

Haven immediately went to Maren and put her paws on Maren's feet.

Maren reached down and scrubbed the dog behind the ears. "Good girl. I'm glad you're okay, too."

From his truck, he could hear Rusk barking. The dog had to be frantic with worry.

"Come on, let's get you into my vehicle," he said to Maren. "We can call this into the local dispatch and for a tow truck for your vehicle. I don't like being out here. We're too exposed."

With a nod, Maren reached back into the Bronco, grabbing a backpack from the passenger's floorboard.

Colt led the way back to his truck while he made the call to the local dispatch, promising them they'd give statements once they were safe.

Keeping an eye out for any more trouble, he opened the back hatch to comfort his K-9. "Do you think Haven would be okay in the back with Rusk?"

Maren seemed to contemplate the question. "If it's okay with you, I'd like to keep her up front with me. We need to let the dogs officially greet each other before we just throw them into an enclosed space. Haven can be an alpha when she needs to."

That brought a smile to Colt. "Rusk is an alpha, too. We'll see how they do when we get to where we're going."

"Which is?"

"Go ahead and get in and I'll tell you."

They climbed into his truck. Once they were both settled, with Haven folding herself onto the seat and putting her head into Maren's lap, Colt said, "First stop the local PD, then Denver. We should go to your task force headquarters."

"I'm good with that."

"I'm sure your boss will want to know this latest development. We need to let him know that your investigation has heated up."

With a gasp, she grasped his arm. "This isn't about the adoption ring. The man with the gun said, '*You should have stayed dead. No one crosses Shadow and lives.*'"

Colt's hands gripped and re-gripped the steering wheel as he drove them away. "The shooter believes you're Opal. This has to do with the drug trafficker. But why shoot at you at the clinic?"

"The shooter must have mistaken me for Opal then, too." Her voice took on a grim edge. "Could this Shadow person have tried to kill her and make it look like a suicide, but she survived and went into hiding?"

"Maybe Opal suspected she was pregnant and wanted out from under Shadow's thumb, so she faked her death to protect her child." Colt's mind whirred with possibilities.

"That would make sense. Especially if she can identify Shadow. We have to find my sister before Shadow does," Maren insisted.

Colt wouldn't lose sight of his mission. "And take down Shadow."

"The task force could help," she said.

"What if Shadow has some connection to the illegal adoption ring the task force is hunting?" Colt turned the thought over in his head. "Your sister shows up at an OB clinic and you're investigating dirty OB's."

"It's something to consider," Maren replied. "We could talk with my boss about it." She went quiet for a moment. "I keep thinking about Opal and what she must be going through. How alone she must feel. I want a second chance with my sister and my baby niece or nephew. I need a second chance."

At the mention of her meeting Opal's baby, his mind went to his own twin nieces. He loved his siblings and their kids, and though he hadn't seen much of them lately because he'd been so focused on taking down Shadow, he couldn't imagine life without his family.

"We'll get Shadow and bring your sister home to you," he vowed.

"Thanks. As much as I want to believe we will succeed, I know better than to hope."

"Sometimes all we have is hope and faith." Colt's hands flexed on the steering wheel. A truth he'd once rejected. But now, every day, he'd found his faith reawakening.

"I agree, in theory. It's just hard sometimes to believe in faith and hope when there's so much bad in the world." Maren petted Haven, her hands working over the sleek Doberman's coat. "For a long time, it was just Opal and me. And then she disappeared. But at least I knew she was alive, and I had hope we'd reconnect. Then trying to accept she was dead…it broke my heart."

It didn't sound like she had much family around. Who did she turn to for support? He couldn't imagine being that alone, and found himself saying, "You must have people who care for you… You're part of an elite federal task force. Surely, you've made friends among your colleagues."

"I'm just starting to get to know the other task force members," she said. "There is one member, Eli Blackwood. We have a bond of shared grief. But I'm not sure that's enough to build a friendship on."

He pulled into the local police department parking lot, thankful to have the distraction of giving their statements and arranging for a tow of Maren's vehicle to the task force headquarters in Denver.

Once they were back on the road, and the miles stretched out, taking them farther away from Barren Valley toward Denver, Maren seemed to grow restless in the passenger seat.

Finally, she broke the silence. "I still have trouble reconciling the sister I knew with a woman who'd be involved with drug dealers. I hadn't realized how far she'd become embroiled in the drug scene. And to date someone high up in the food chain—what was she thinking?"

"People can hide who they are until it's too late and you're in too deep," he replied.

"Sounds like you're speaking from experience."

"Unfortunately, I am." He wasn't sure he wanted to go down this road, but here they were and for some reason he felt the need to tell her. "My last serious relationship ended on a very sour note."

"I'm sorry to hear that," she murmured. "Did she break your heart?"

"Not only my heart but the law," he replied. The old anger tinged his tone. He'd been so blinded by his love for Rebecca. A fate he swore to himself he'd never allow again. "She was dealing drugs right under my nose."

"Whoa."

"Yeah. Whoa." A shudder worked over him. "I had to arrest her and now she's doing time."

"That's rough. And I thought my love life was dismal," Maren stated with a grim tone.

He gave her a questioning glance, inviting her to speak further. But she remained quiet.

Apparently, she wouldn't be sharing.

An awkward tension settled over the cab and he wasn't sure what to say next. Finally, she broke the silence. "Well, you know about me and Opal. What's your family like?"

That was a safer topic. "I come from a big clan of includers. It wouldn't be a gathering at my parents' without a slew of guests we've all collected. I'm a middle child. Two older siblings, one sister and one brother. And two younger siblings, also a brother and sister. Comes with a lot of drama, a lot of laughter and a lot of tears."

"That sounds wonderful."

Her wistful note had his heart contracting.

"Hey, you'll have a niece or nephew to love on soon," he told her. "I have twin nieces. And a couple of nephews who are rowdy with a capital *R*."

They shared a smile. A dimple winked at him from one corner of her mouth. His heart did a little thump. So pretty.

Warmth gathered in his chest. Unnerved by his attraction to Maren, who was impressive while drawing him in at the same time, Colt concentrated on the road.

The woman next to him was equal parts tough cop and loving sister. But his trust level was low ever since he was betrayed by a woman who turned out to be in the drug trade. He still beat himself up that he hadn't known until the day he'd had to arrest her. She'd broken his faith and his heart.

His faith was slowly being restored, but his heart—not so much.

And if he wasn't careful, this woman beside him could work her way through the cracks of the barricades he'd erected to keep from ever experiencing the kind of pain he had with Rebecca.

If he were to let Maren in, would there be healing? Or just more heartache in store for him?

Not questions he wanted to spend any energy on finding the answers to.

Two hours later, Colt brought his truck to a halt in the parking lot of the Colorado K-9 Unit task force headquarters building. A two story-brick building with lots of windows.

"The bottom floor is our training center," Maren said. "Upstairs are the offices."

Curious to see the task force's digs, Colt jumped out and

released Rusk from the back of the truck. Once the dog was leashed and Maren had Haven on a lead, Colt and Rusk walked next to Maren and Haven toward to the building. Maren led them around to the back to a lawn surrounded by a short fence. Once inside the gated area, Maren removed Haven's lead. Colt followed suit.

"Playtime," Maren said with a smile.

The dogs hesitated, then slowly walked in opposite directions before circling back to sniff each other.

Haven bowed, the signal for play. Then she and Rusk were running around the grassy space, taking turns chasing each other.

"I think they'll get along," Colt said.

"Agreed." She whistled.

Haven immediately veered in an arc and ran back to Maren's side.

Rusk stood still for a moment as if confused by the other dog's desertion.

"Here," Colt called out.

Rusk raced to his side.

Once they had the dogs back on their leashes, they headed for the building. The training center of the federal building had a large, enclosed ring with ramps, tunnels and window cutouts for training. Kennels lined one wall.

"Hey, Maren," a man in his sixties approached. He was tall and fit, with salt-and-pepper hair, a dark beard and mustache. He wore a green polo shirt with the task force logo on the breast pocket and khaki pants.

"Good afternoon, Dev." Maren gestured to Colt. "This is DEA Agent Colt Dawson. Colt, Dev Singh, our lead trainer. Though he's retiring soon."

Colt shook the man's hand. "Nice to meet you."

"Likewise." Dev's focus turned to Rusk. "Hello, handsome." To Colt, he said, "Can I?"

Colt nodded his permission for Dev to interact with his partner. "This is Rusk."

Dev crouched and let Rusk sniff his hand before scrubbing the dog behind the ears. "Will you two be joining our training today?"

Haven pushed forward for some pets. Dev laughed and scrubbed her behind the ears with one hand while also scrubbing Rusk. Colt was glad to see the two K-9s sharing. It meant they wouldn't be as likely to resource guard if they spent more time together.

Maren shook her head. "We're here to talk to Emmett. Can we leave the dogs down here for a bit?"

"Of course." Dev stood and swept a hand toward the row of crates. "Pick any kennel."

A high-pitched yapping had Colt spinning in time to see two German shepherd puppies run into the ring. Another trainer who looked to be in her late teens, wearing the same sort of outfit as Dev, hurried behind them.

"Those two are running me ragged," the young woman said as she shooed the puppies into the ring and shut the gate.

"Hi, Jessie," Maren made the introduction. "Jessie is a part-time high school volunteer."

With a wave, Jessie slipped into the arena to chase after the pups.

Colt smiled at the young woman. "Is it normal for that one pup to have a bent ear?"

"No," Dev answered. "We're hopeful Trooper's ear will straighten as he ages. These two are brothers donated by Dodger Andrews."

Colt recognized the last name. The man was a benefactor of K-9 training programs in the area. "Any relation to the missing pregnant woman?"

"Her grandfather," Maren supplied.

After settling their K-9 partners into separate crates, Colt followed Maren up a couple of flights of stairs to an office area. A large conference room sat off to one side with a huge screen dominating one wall. A long oval table and multiple chairs stood waiting.

Maren headed down a hallway to an office, prompting Colt to keep up. The nameplate on the door read FBI Supervisory Special Agent Emmett Dane.

She knocked and then stepped inside.

A tall, broad-shouldered man rose from behind his desk. Serious blue eyes regarded them with surprise. “Maren, I wasn’t expecting you.”

Maren moved forward. “Emmett, this is DEA Agent Colt Dawson.”

Colt shook hands with Emmett.

“Your boss speaks highly of you,” Emmett said. “Glad to meet you.”

Emmett turned to Maren. “How’s the search for your sister going?”

She explained about the attack on her vehicle and what the gunman had said before Colt shot him and he fled.

Emmett rubbed his chin, his gaze on Maren. “It’s safe to surmise this Shadow believes that you are your sister.”

“That’s what we’re thinking,” Colt confirmed.

With a nod, Emmett leaned a hip on his desk. “Shadow’s men may come after you again.”

“We’ll be ready for them,” Maren assured her boss.

Colt liked that she included him in her statement.

“Is there any reason to suspect Shadow is involved in the illegal adoption ring?” Emmett asked.

“I wouldn’t put it past Shadow,” Colt stated.

“Okay, then stick close together.” Emmett glanced at Colt. “I’ll talk to your boss about bringing you on to the task force.”

Not sure he was understanding, Colt questioned, “You want me on the task force?”

"We're using every available resource to track down the villains who are dealing in the buying and selling of babies and if your case can help us solve our case, then that's what we'll do."

"I'm glad to help if I can," Colt said. "But my mission is to find the drug kingpin."

"I have faith you can accomplish what you set out to," Emmett said. He shifted his focus to Maren. "Concentrate on finding your sister. You said the clinic receptionist mentioned Derek Rolls had a wife?"

Maren nodded. "She couldn't remember her name, only that she seemed like a timid woman."

Emmett frowned. "I'll put Eli on tracking down Mrs. Rolls. Good work, Maren."

"The informant who gave you information about my sister," Maren said to Colt. "He's in Denver, correct?"

"He is," Colt confirmed, wondering where she was going with the question.

Emmett stood. "Have Eva do research for this informant as well as any information she can get on Opal's whereabouts. If there is a connection between Shadow and our baby smuggling ring, I want to know about it. Mia Andrews is counting on us to find her."

Thinking of the missing pregnant teen that Maren had told him about, Colt fisted his hands. "Of course. If my hunt for Shadow leads us to Mia and helps bust the adoption ring, all the better."

"Including bringing my sister back safely," Maren added.

They bid the FBI agent goodbye, then Maren led the way to Eva Gomez's office. The task force's tech analyst's domain was a hub of electronics. A pretty woman sat at a bank of computers. Her long, wavy hair was captured in a clip at her nape. She turned dark eyes on them as they approached. "Well, to what do I owe the pleasure?"

"Hi, Eva, this is DEA Agent Colt Dawson. He's working

with us on a possible connected case," Maren said, briefing Eva on what they suspected. "We need some information on one of his CIs."

Colt gave the woman the name of his confidential informant. "Steve Loren. The guy sent me looking for Opal at the motel in Barren Valley. He's one of Shadow's minions but apparently had a soft spot for Opal."

"I'm on it." Eva spun back to her keyboard; her fingers flew over black keys. An image popped up on the computer screen with a long rap sheet.

"Yep, that's him," Colt affirmed.

"Can you send me that address?" Maren said.

Eva's fingers worked quickly. "Done."

"Thanks," Maren said. "We appreciate you."

Colt and Maren made their way back to the training center to release their K-9s from their kennels.

"Do you think Steve will cooperate?" Maren asked as they climbed into his truck.

"That will depend on if he's more afraid of us or Shadow," Colt told her.

His pulse thrummed at the thought that they were now officially working together. Teammates. He would have to make sure to keep a professional distance, because anything else would only end in disaster.

FIVE

With Haven and Rusk secure in the back compartment of Colt's truck, Maren sat in the passenger seat while Colt drove them to the address provided by Eva for Steve Loren, Colt's CI.

They entered a seedy neighborhood of Aurora, a suburb of Denver. Run-down redbrick apartment buildings lined the street with overgrown common spaces in between.

Alert for any threats. Maren's heart rate remained high after having her tire blown out and a masked gunman pointing his rifle at her.

The gunman had thought she was Opal. Bile seared her throat.

Her sister was being hunted by the drug kingpin known as Shadow, as well as the DEA. One wanted her dead, and the other wanted her help in taking down the former. Both put her sister in a precarious, dangerous position.

A position Maren had trained for, but not her sister. Opal wouldn't survive without help. Maren slanted a sideways glance at Colt, taking in the strong lines and angles of his handsome face. She wanted to dislike the man, but there was something about him… She blew out a breath.

The dark slash of his eyebrows over green eyes and the close-cropped beard couldn't diminish the strength in the cut of his jaw, nor could the mustache conceal the fine shape of his lips.

She forced her gaze away from his too handsome face, noting the capable way his hands held the steering wheel at ten and two. He was solid and steadfast. Trustworthy.

Trust didn't come easy. Allowing anyone close was something she avoided. Yet, even though she'd only known him for such a short time, she unexpectedly trusted him, which wasn't something she took lightly.

Nor the fact he'd saved her life.

Gratitude filled her chest. If he hadn't been following her when the gunman in the van had shot out her tire and sent her into the ditch… If Colt hadn't managed to chase off the gunman—a shudder worked over her. She was thankful to be alive. And it was all due to this man beside her. She owed him, but was the cost going to be her sister's life?

And now Maren and Colt were officially working together. Partners.

Somehow this partnership was different than those she'd formed with the Colorado K-9 Unit task force members. The other K-9 officers and their leader, Emmett, all had a common goal to find Mia Andrews and bring to justice the malicious criminals killing young women and selling their babies.

A worthy mission.

When she'd received the notice to report to the task force headquarters in Denver, she'd been both surprised and flattered. It had been an honor to be included and deputized as a federal agent with all the perks and responsibility that went with the designation.

Of course, she realized Haven was a big part of the equation. The dog was good at her job.

All the dogs on the task force were good at their jobs. And the handlers all exceptional in their respective departments.

She was sure Colt and Rusk were good at their job.

They both had a vested interest in finding Opal, even if they'd started out with different motivations. And now their purposes were aligned. What had Opal done to enrage Shadow?

Was the fact she knew his face enough for him to want her dead? Where was she now? Was Opal pregnant? And scared enough to fake her own death?

The questions spun through Maren's brain like the wheel on the TV show *Wheel of Fortune*. She wondered what answers they would learn when they found Steve Loren.

He had to be able to lead her to her sister.

Please, Jesus, I need to find her.

She knew Colt's goal was to take down Shadow. She wanted that as well, since the man was trying to kill her sister. And because his henchmen thought she was Opal, they'd nearly killed her.

Colt parallel parked the truck between two cars, barely managing to fit in the tight space. Maren had to admit she was thankful that her boss had brought Colt onto the team for now and that he had given them permission to follow this lead.

So that she could find her sister. Not because she felt safe with Colt at her side.

Guilt stabbed at her for not pursuing the illegal baby adoption ring. But finding Opal could lead to the OB or other adoption ring members who could crack the case.

Worry for Mia Andrews still took up residence in her brain. She lifted up another silent prayer that Mia would be found soon.

Along with Opal.

Maren felt bad for Dodger Andrews because not knowing where a loved one had disappeared to was torture.

Colt turned off the engine. "You ready for this?"

His question triggered her defensiveness. "Of course."

Was he suggesting she wasn't up to the task of finding her sister? Did he view her as less than because she was only an officer rather than a full-fledged federal agent?

Her rational brain reeled her back from the edge. She purposely relaxed the fists she'd made.

No need to snap at the man. He was helping her, even if doing so furthered his own investigation.

She hated that her first reaction to any sort of perceived judgment was to lash out. It was because people underestimated her all the time due to her looks. In some situations, her silly dimples and unassuming demeanor worked to her advantage, but she didn't want Colt to believe she wasn't good at her job.

She met his green-eyed gaze, liking the way the edges of his irises were rimmed with a darker color, and was suddenly aware of an unwanted attraction zinging through her veins.

Stay on point, she admonished herself and jerked her gaze away. "Sorry, I'm on edge."

"Understandable," he said and popped open his door.

They climbed out of the truck and released the dogs from the back compartment. Both K-9s were well trained and sat next to their partners until they were leashed.

With silent agreement, Maren and Colt led the dogs to a patch of sparse grass and weeds so they could see to their needs, before heading into the apartment building where Steve lived on the fifth floor.

The inside of the building was as run-down as the outside. The walls were dingy, and several light fixtures were broken. Caution tape across the elevator sent them to the stairs. A musty odor had all of them sneezing. They reached the fifth floor and stepped out into the hallway.

A couple of teenagers were hanging out near an open apartment door. When they saw Colt and Maren they disappeared inside and slammed the door shut.

"We have to make this quick," Colt said. "I'm sure the gossip train will be announcing our presence within seconds."

She nodded and tucked her jacket behind her sidearm. She wanted nothing to get in the way if she needed to defend herself and Haven. She glanced at Colt and wanted to assure him she was up to whatever they would face. "I have your back."

He smiled, lighting up his whole face. Her heart did a little bump. "And I have yours."

They found Steve's apartment at the end of the hall. Colt knocked. A faint rustling could be heard from inside the apartment.

Maren hung back so that when Steve looked through the peephole, he'd only see Colt. She didn't want to spook the man.

The door was yanked open. "What are you doing here?"

Steve had a gravelly voice. The stench of burnt cabbage wafted out the open door.

"We need to talk." Colt and Rusk stepped into the apartment, forcing Steve to back up.

Maren and Haven filled the space behind Colt and Rusk. She shut the door behind her, locking it. Rusk sniffed the ground and then stood still, his body pointing toward a black lacquered cabinet against the wall. Haven lifted her nose, her ears twitching. She strained at her lead but Maren kept her close despite the obvious signs of alert to drugs in the apartment.

Steve was a wiry guy with greasy hair. He wore baggy sweat bottoms and a misbuttoned plaid shirt. His feet were bare. His gray eyes grew round as he stared at Maren. "Oh no. No, no, no."

He put his hands up in the air like he wanted to ward her off while his gaze darted everywhere as if looking for an escape. "Why did you bring her here? You were supposed to save her, not drag her and her mess into my world."

Maren stepped forward. Haven sniffed the air and let out a bark. She was alerting. There were definitely drugs in the apartment.

Rewarding her dog's reaction with a treat, she asked Steve, "How did you know Opal would be in Barren Valley?"

Steve tucked in his chin, a frown deepening the lines in his forehead. His beady gray eyes landed on her again. "Hey, hey, hey. Who are you? You look like Opal."

Choosing not to answer the question, Maren said, "You answer my question first."

Steve backed up toward the window. "Man, you two shouldn't be here. Were you followed?"

He peered out the window and jumped back. "If Shadow catches wind you're here, I'm dead. You got to leave. I don't know who you are, and I don't want to know." He jerked his gaze to Colt. "I gave you a chance to save Opal. If you didn't take it, that's on you."

Colt and Rusk moved, circling behind Steve and pushing him toward Maren. Haven stepped in front of Maren.

Steve held up his hands again. His gaze darting to the dog, to Colt and then to Maren. "I don't want any part of this."

"But you *are* a part of it," Colt said. "How did you know Opal Anderson would be in Barren Valley?"

Steve chopped his hands in the air. "If I tell you, I'm a dead man."

"We can protect you," Maren assured him in a tone she used for children and animals.

"Who are you?" Steve asked again.

Wanting to stop this circling of the conversation, Maren said, "I'm Opal's sister. And I'm with the Colorado Springs PD."

Steve noisily inhaled. "Not cool." He spun to look at Colt. "Talking to you was bad enough. Shadow's got people in the PD."

"In which PD?" Colt asked.

Steve shrugged. "I don't know."

Maren's heart dropped. "Do you know who?"

"Naw, man. Shadow only tells what he wants to tell. He tests everybody. I bet me learning he knew Opal was in Barren Valley was a test." Steve's face fell. "I failed it. But I couldn't let him kill Opal. She's good people. A little lost. Especially now that Georgy's dead."

"Who's Georgy?" Maren asked. "Is he the father of her baby?"

Steve eyes widened. "I don't know anything about a baby."

Maren winced inwardly at having just revealed her sister's pregnancy to this man. Though she assumed he already knew, which was why he'd tried to help her in the first place. If Shadow did get to him and he told, what then? Her stomach muscles clenched with dread. Was Shadow involved in the illegal baby ring?

"I just know Georgy was tight with Shadow," Steve continued. "But he and Opal, they wanted out. They wanted to skip town and go far away." He nodded, his brown hair flopping over his forehead. "Makes sense if they were expecting. The only way out would be if they were dead."

Hearing this only confirmed for Maren that Opal had faked her death because she thought it the only way to get out from under Shadow's thumb.

"What do you know about Vinnie Homer?" Colt asked.

Recognizing the name of the person who'd witnessed Opal's supposed drowning, Maren waited for Steve's answer, her breath stalling.

Steve made a face. "Not much. I only met him once. He was pals with Georgy. Twitchy guy."

Maren's insides twisted with worry. She thought Steve was twitchy and he considered Vinnie twitchy? That didn't bode well. "Do you know where Opal is now? Shadow's men tried to kill her in Barren Valley." She didn't add that they almost took her out instead.

"No, lady," Steve said. "I haven't heard anything more. If I go back to Shadow now, I'm as good as dead, I tell you. I need to skip town." He looked to Colt and held out his hand. "You gotta give me some money to get a bus out of town. Or better yet, the train. I've never been on a train."

"Tell me where to find Shadow and I will," Colt said.

Steve dropped his hand. "You don't find Shadow..." His tone dripped with mockery. "Shadow finds you. That's why they call him Shadow."

Irritation crawled up her spine and she stepped closer. Haven moved as well, matching Maren's step. The dog's posture was one of readiness in case Steve decided to become a threat. Haven wouldn't hesitate to sink her teeth into his flesh. "He has to have a base of operation."

Steve swallowed, visibly frightened by the dog. Yet, he was smart enough to stay still. "If he does, I don't know it. He shows up when least expected."

"Where's the last place you saw him?" Colt asked.

"He came round last week," Steve said. "I'm not the only guy in this building who runs errands for Shadow."

"You mean runs drugs," Colt said.

Steve frowned, then perked up. "The park. I forgot. I got a message to be there." Eyeing both dogs with wariness, Steve hustled over to a coffee table and picked a piece of paper. He offered it to Colt. "I'm not showing my face there. Or anywhere. I'm afraid he knows I told you where Opal was. I haven't left my apartment in days."

Maren shared a glance with Colt. This was his CI after all. "What do you think we should do?"

Colt seemed to contemplate the question, and then to Steve, he said, "Pack a bag. You're coming with us."

Maren raised her eyebrows. "And just where is he going to sit?"

Colt's mouth stretched into a mischievous smile. "With the dogs, of course."

Maren pressed her lips together to keep from laughing. The image of Steve hunkered down into the back of the dog compartment with Haven and Rusk was comical. But she wasn't sure that would be appropriate. They wouldn't want to be accused of mistreating him. "Can you contact someone in the DEA and have them pick him up and taken to a safe house?"

Clearly feigning disappointment, Colt shrugged. "Yeah, that's plan B. They'll also do a sweep of the place."

Maren shook her head and couldn't keep the small smile from breaking through. She hadn't considered Colt might have a sense of humor.

"You two got to believe me, if anybody sees you here—" He made a cutting gesture with his finger across his throat.

Thinking of the two teenagers who had been in the hallway when they stepped out of the stairwell, Maren said, "It may be too late to keep our visit a secret. We should call for a police presence. We'll arrest you. That way we can take you out without any hassle."

"That's a brilliant plan." Colt stepped forward, pulling Steve's arms behind his back and handcuffing him.

"Hey, hey, hey," Steve protested.

"Do you want to make the call?" Colt asked Maren.

"If Shadow does have somebody in the police department, it'd be better if you reach out to your agency," she said.

"Copy." Colt stepped away and made the call. He returned and said, "Fifteen minutes out."

"That fast?" Maren said.

"Apparently a team raided a warehouse not far from here," Colt said. "They're wrapping up. A few arrests and some drugs confiscated."

Maren's pulse jumped. "Shadow?"

"Hard to say since nobody knows what he looks like." Colt looked at Steve speculatively. "But you can identify him."

"We need you to give a description," Maren said.

Steve shook his head. "Naw, man. He always wears a mask. He don't want no one to see his face."

Could one of the masked men who'd run her off the road have been Shadow? Maren tried to remember the height and build of the man who'd broken out her car window, but all she could see when she thought back to that moment was the business end of an automatic weapon. "Have you heard any rumors about Shadow being hurt?"

Steve shook his head. "Like I said, I haven't poked my head out in days."

"Do you know his real name?" Colt asked.

Steve scoffed. "Only those in the inner circle know. Maybe."

Frustration beat a steady rhythm in Maren's brain.

"While we're here, let's have the dogs search the place," Colt said.

"Man, this is bogus," Steve said. "You got no cause."

Maren pointed a finger at him. "You'd rather we leave you to Shadow?"

Steve blanched. "No." He gave a resigned sigh. "Whatever."

Maren and Colt unleashed the dogs and gave the search command. Within seconds both dogs zeroed in on the black cabinet. Inside the cabinet were little pills packaged in plastic and sealed with duct tape.

Taking a picture of the stash of what she assumed to be opioids with her phone, and sending it to Colt, Maren said, "Steve, you're under arrest."

Fifteen minutes later, DEA agents swarmed the neighborhood. Colt recognized most of them but he wasn't close to any of his fellow agents. Several Aurora and Denver police cruisers arrived as well. While Maren went to talk to the local law enforcement officers, Colt and Rusk walked Steve out of the building, placing him into the back of a black SUV.

When Maren joined him on the sidewalk, he could read the upset on her face. "What gives?"

"The local LEOs are mad that we didn't call the PD first to make the arrest," she said. "I told them this was the DEA's op and that you and I are part of Colorado K-9 Unit task force."

"Good thinking," Colt said, admiring her mental acuity.

"Not sure it mollified them," she said. "They wanted to know why we were chasing down drug dealers when the task force was formed to stop the illegal baby adoption ring."

He could tell the conversation had her wound up tight. "If Shadow is as plugged into the criminal element in Colorado as I believe he is, he may know something useful. All the more reason we need to bring him into custody."

Maren's gaze narrowed. "One of my priorities is finding my sister and keeping her alive."

Colt acknowledged her words with a nod. "Of course. We can do both."

"Just so you know, if it comes down to a choice of taking in Shadow or protecting my sister, I'll choose my sister," Maren said, her voice hard. "What will you choose?"

His gut twisted. He didn't like being put on the spot. For too long he'd been after Shadow. The criminal had proved elusive, and for Colt, the hunt bordered on obsession driven by the overdose death of his cousin. Colt's determination was what made him a good agent. At least, that was what his boss told him. He didn't know if he could let an opportunity to take the criminal down slip by.

When he remained silent, Maren asked, "Why are you so hot to bring Shadow down? This feels personal."

He sucked in a breath. He glanced around at the remaining DEA agents who were bringing out the stash of opioids and putting them into a compartment in another black SUV. There were tons of gawkers from the neighboring buildings crowding the sidewalks and window frames. Any one of them could be Shadow. Or working for the drug kingpin. "Personal. Yes, very."

"And?" she prompted. "The least you can do is tell me why."

Glancing around again, wondering who might hear and who might be a threat, he shook his head. "Not here."

She took in a breath, obviously reining in her frustration. "Fine. But I'm not going to let you squirm out of spilling the truth."

No, she wouldn't. He'd already discovered she was tenacious. Good trait in a law enforcement officer. "I wouldn't dream of it."

DEA Agent Daniel Russell came up to Colt. He wore a dark suit with a shoulder holster visible beneath his jacket. His thick brown hair was swept off his high forehead. His gaze flicked to Maren and lingered.

A strange irritation invaded Colt. He didn't like the interested look on Daniel's face. But he couldn't blame the other man—Maren was gorgeous and fierce and so smart.

Colt mentally reared back from the direction his thoughts were headed. Falling back on the manners his mother taught him, he said, "Daniel, this is Officer Maren Anderson of the Colorado Springs Police Department." He refrained from mentioning the task force because the info wasn't relative to the investigation into Shadow.

Daniel inclined his head. "Officer." Turning back to Colt he said, "We're done here. Thanks for the tip. I'll take it from here."

"You know what to do," Colt said, shaking the man's hand. They'd already had a confidential conversation about placing Steve in a safe house until they could bring in Shadow.

"Out of sight, out of mind." With one last glance at Maren, Daniel headed to the SUV where Steve Loren sat in the back.

Once the black SUV took off and the police presence dispersed, Colt cupped Maren's elbow and steered her toward his truck. "We should get out of here, too."

With the dogs leading the way, Colt and Maren moved in tandem, hurrying to where'd he'd parked his rig.

From behind them, a man shouted, "Opal?"

When Maren would have turned, Colt squeezed her elbow, "Keep going. Hurry."

Soon they were urging the dogs into a run.

The sound of pounding feet echoed off the brick buildings. Both Maren and Colt skidded to a halt and turned to assess the oncoming threat. Two men ran toward them. Neither wore a mask, which led him to believe maybe they lived in the building but were working for Shadow.

"They think I'm Opal," Maren stage-whispered. "We can't let them realize I'm not. But they'll think she's working with law enforcement."

Agreeing with a nod, he yanked open the passenger door. "Get in."

Maren dove into the passenger seat. "Haven, come."

Without hesitation, Haven jumped into the cab of the truck, settling in the space on the bench seat next to Maren.

Rusk let out a bark.

"Rusk, come." Maren patted her lap.

As if seeking permission, Rusk looked at Colt.

Urgency making his voice harsh, Colt commanded, "In."

Rusk leaped onto Maren's lap. Her arms circled around him.

Colt slammed the door shut.

As the two men ran up to the truck, Colt placed his hand on his sidearm but noticed both men's hands were empty. No guns. Good.

He contemplated drawing his weapon and demanding information on Shadow, but the sidewalk seemed suddenly very crowded as more men from the buildings on both sides of the street moved toward him.

Releasing his weapon, he rounded the truck and got into the driver's seat and started the engine. One of the men stepped in front of the truck as if to prevent Colt from leaving, but he revved the engine and eased forward, forcing the man to jump out of the way before Colt stepped on the gas and, in a squeal of tires, drove the truck down the street.

He looked in the rearview mirror to see one of the men already on a cell phone. No doubt telling their boss, Shadow, they'd just seen Opal Anderson driving away in a brown truck.

They were going to have to get new wheels. Fast.

SIX

Gripping the door handle, Maren kept an eye on the passenger side-view mirror, checking to see if they were being followed. Anxiousness cut through her like a toothy saw. Someone had recognized her. Or rather, thought they'd recognized Opal, and had chased her and Colt down the street on the heels of a DEA arrest of one of Shadow's dealers. Now Shadow and his fellow criminals would wonder if Opal was cooperating with the feds. Another reason for Shadow to want to eliminate Opal.

Better for the men to think she was Opal than for them to realize their mistake and go looking for her sister, who was out there somewhere, alone and defenseless. How scared she must be.

Helpless worry chomped through Maren. She wanted her sister home safe.

She shot a glance at Colt, behind the wheel of his unassuming truck. She was glad the two dogs were riding so well together with Haven crouched on the seat beside her and Rusk now sitting on the floor at her feet with her backpack.

"We need to find Vinnie, the witness," she said, grasping for something tangible to help her find her sister. "He must know Opal didn't really drown. He might know where she'd go."

Maren hoped he'd have answers because she was at a loss. For too long, Opal had cut Maren out of her life, kept her at a distance. Despite being twins, Maren had no idea where her sister would seek refuge. With their parents and uncle gone, they had no other family. Not knowing whom her sister would turn to signaled how much they'd grown apart, and the lack of closeness between them filled Maren with sadness.

"Agreed." Colt flicked on the blinker and headed the truck up the ramp for the freeway that would take them back to Colorado Springs. The truck ate up the miles.

Maren concentrated on her breathing as they drew closer to her hometown.

Colt's cell phone rang, cutting into the silence. He hit the button on the steering wheel and connected the call. "Dawson, go."

"Hey, Colt," a disembodied voice echoed through the cab. "Henry Spares here."

Haven's ears twitched. Rusk's head swiveled toward Colt. "I wanted to follow up with you on that information you gave Daniel about Shadow having a rendezvous in the Aurora Park," Henry said, his voice low and smooth. "No one showed. But two undercover agents are staking out the park for the rest of the afternoon, just in case."

Colt let out a heavy sigh that Maren felt in her chest. "Doubtful Shadow will show now. Not after realizing one of his gophers has been scooped up."

"Roger that," Henry said. "Your CI is securely ensconced in a safe house miles from Aurora."

"Good." Colt glanced at Maren. The speculation in his eyes had her curious. What was he thinking? She had a hard time reading him and that left her a bit off-kilter.

"See if you can get any more information out of him," Colt said. "I think he told us everything he knew but I can't be certain. He says he only saw Shadow with a mask on. But maybe he can describe the guy's eyes. Not sure how helpful the description would be, but you never know."

"On it," the agent said. "I know a forensic artist who can work with such limited info."

Ah. Good thinking on Colt's part. Sometimes a little went a long way.

"We're headed to Colorado Springs to look for the man who came forward as a witness to Opal Anderson's death," Colt told Henry before signing off.

"I'll have Eva find us his address." Maren pulled out her cell phone and dialed the task force's main line.

Her call was answered on the fourth ring. "Eva Gomez," the tech analyst said. "What can I help you with?"

"Eva, it's Maren. I need the last-known address of a Vinnie Homer. I don't have my sister's case file with me so I can't get it. I'm hoping you can help with this."

"Of course," Eva said. The clicking of keys on a keyboard clanged in Maren's ears, making her realize she had a headache brewing. She pushed the speaker button so she could hold the phone at a distance.

"It says here he's living in a homeless encampment," Eva said.

"There are encampments all around the area." Maren grimaced. "It'll be like looking for a needle among a ton of haystacks."

Eva made a noise of agreement. "Do you need a photo?"

"I do. Please text it to me," Maren said.

"Done."

Maren's phone dinged with an incoming text.

"Let me know if you need anything else," Eva said before clicking off.

"Sounds like we have our work cut out for us," Colt said, pointing out the obvious.

"Just like everything else with my sister, nothing is easy," Maren admitted. Something she didn't voice often about her twin. "Opal always seemed to have a cloud hanging over her. Even when we were kids, she struggled with things that came much easier for me. I never understood why."

"Everyone's journey is different," Colt said.

There was truth in his statement. "Tell me why bringing down Shadow is so personal for you."

Colt gripped the steering wheel so hard his knuckles turned white. Maren wondered what nerve she'd hit.

"When I was sixteen, my eighteen-year-old cousin got hooked on drugs. Back then, crack cocaine and heroin were the most prevalent drugs on the street."

Maren's heart contracted with empathy. "I'm sorry to hear that. It must've been difficult for you and your family."

"Devastating," Colt said. "No matter how much we tried to intervene, he couldn't shake the addiction."

Maren sucked in a breath. She sensed there was a tragic ending to the story but she charged ahead. "Was he ever able to beat it?"

She waited, her breath stalled in her lungs, hoping his cousin had tamed the addiction because she needed to hope that Opal could tame hers.

"No." Colt's voice was soft and filled with anguish. "I found him in his parents' backyard. A needle stuck in his arm. He'd overdosed on tainted heroin."

Even though she'd expected that outcome, grief for him and his family made her heart ache. Unable to stop herself, she reached out and put a hand on his shoulder. The muscles beneath her palm were rock-hard. There was a solidity to him that she found appealing. "I'm so sad that happened to you."

He released his right hand from the steering wheel and placed it over hers on his shoulder. The warmth of his skin on hers rippled through her. His touch was sure, yet gentle. Comforting, despite the fact she was supposed to be comforting him.

"Thank you. I swore that day I was going to do everything I could to stop the drugs from flowing into my city," he said. "As soon as I graduated from college, I entered the police academy. I was on the job for eight years with the Denver PD before moving to the DEA. Then two years ago I trained to have Rusk," he said. "He's been the best partner."

Maren released his shoulder, but he kept her from slipping her hand away with a slight squeeze before he let go and regripped the steering wheel. She folded her hands in her lap, but the warmth of his touch remained imprinted on her skin. Haven, tucked in the space between them on the bench seat, rested her snout on her hands.

"There's something both comforting and thrilling about a working dog as a partner." She smoothed her hand over Haven's short fur.

"True," Colt said. "Rusk kept me from going dark when the whole thing with Rebecca blew up."

With her other hand, she scratched Rusk behind the ears where he sat at her feet.

For a long moment, they were both quiet.

"I get why you went into law enforcement," she stated softly, her heart aching for his loss. "But surely Shadow wasn't active when you were sixteen?"

No matter how strong, capable and brave Colt may have been at the beginning of his career, filled with aspirations of removing drugs from the street so people like his cousin wouldn't lose their way, she hated to think of him going up against someone as notorious and dangerous as Shadow alone. Even with the backing of the DEA, he was on a one-man-and-dog crusade.

She was determined to make sure they all survived.

Colt sighed. Going down this road would be painful. But he couldn't shy away from the truth. That wouldn't serve any purpose. Better to face it all head-on. "No, he wasn't active when my cousin was alive. I didn't come across Shadow until a few years ago. He's why I became a K-9 handler. I needed a partner to sniff out drugs."

"To stop him."

"In short, yes." For a second, Colt contemplated leaving the story unfinished, but they were partners now. She needed to understand. And for some reason, he felt compelled to explain. "I was mentoring a teen, Tony, through my church on my days off. Good kid but from a chaotic home. Tony swore up and down to me that he wasn't using, yet I saw the signs. He'd come to our meetings jittery and his eyes glassy."

The memory stung. "Yet, when I searched through his things, I came up empty. His parents were negligent in caring for him, being addicted themselves, but without a warrant, I couldn't search their home. One day, Tony didn't show up. Later, I learned he'd fled when a patrol officer saw him buying drugs off a known dealer. The dealer was arrested but Tony ran into traffic and was hit by a car."

Grief was a chain Colt wore around his neck. With each death, the burden grew heavier. "If I had had Rusk with me back then, maybe Tony wouldn't be dead."

"You can't know that for sure," Maren said. "Was Shadow the dealer?"

The anger that had spurred him on rose, burning in his chest. "Even back then, Shadow kept out of sight. But he was the supplier and boss of the dealer. The dealer died in a jail cell waiting for his arraignment."

Maren made a distressed sound that had both dogs shifting closer to her. "You think he had the dealer killed."

"I do. Though how, I don't know." The not knowing kept him up at night.

"Shadow's always been deadly."

"Yes." Acid ate at Colt's gut. Through the rearview mirror he clocked a black truck cruising up fast through traffic. "And ever since then, I've been trying to bring him down."

He shook his head with self-recrimination. "Then there was Rebecca, my ex."

Just saying her name had the volcano of suppressed rage inside of him bubbling. "Rusk never liked her."

"Dogs are good judges of character."

Seeing how Rusk put his head on Maren's knee had Colt's heart softening. "Yes. They are."

Returning his gaze to the road, he steeled himself to share his story. "Rusk barked at her as if telling her off. I thought he was jealous of having to share my attention. Little did I realize he was alerting, just not his normal, passive alert. I don't know how I missed it."

"But you and he weren't working, so a passive alert in that case wouldn't have worked, right? You would have thought he was just sitting nicely, being well-behaved, around this new person," she pointed out.

He hadn't thought about it that way. "You're probably right," he admitted, grateful for her understanding. "Rusk didn't like her the moment I brought her around. She was the first relationship I'd been involved in since I'd become partners with him, so I wasn't prepared for his reaction. I didn't know what to expect."

"The first time for anything is always a learning curve."

"He must've smelled the residue of narcotics even though she didn't have any substances on her. There were times when I thought her behavior was very strange and suspicions flared," he admitted. "I felt guilty for even thinking such thoughts about Rebecca." He shrugged. "I once searched her house and came up empty. I figured I was being paranoid."

"It sounds like a tricky situation. I don't know how I'd react if I were in your shoes."

"How does Haven react to your dat—" Colt cut himself off. He had no business prying into her love life.

"I don't date," she said.

"At all?" He wanted to delve into that tidbit.

She made a noncommittal noise. "Are you keeping an eye on the black truck four cars back?"

Appreciation of her flared. "I am. It's keeping its distance, but we need to ditch my truck and find a new ride."

"Take this next off-ramp," she said. "There's a mall about a half mile up the road with a five-story parking structure. We can lose them there."

At the last second, without signaling, Colt spun the steering wheel, sending the truck across two lanes of traffic. The blare of horns followed them as he shot down the ramp and ran through a red light.

More honking and the screeching of tires behind them had him glancing in the mirror. The black truck had taken the same exit. They were, indeed, being followed.

Racing through traffic like a slot car, he headed to the mall on the left. "Hang on!"

Maren grabbed hold of both dogs' collars and braced her feet on the floorboards. Colt drove the truck into oncoming traffic. She held her breath as cars swerved to avoid being hit. Colt drove masterfully as he maneuvered his truck into the large parking structure. Pedestrians dove out of the way.

Maren murmured under her breath, "Please, Lord, no accidents."

The truck entered the five-story parking structure, and the sudden absence of the June sun had Maren blinking to readjust her eyes to the dim lighting.

In the distance, she heard the blaring of horns. No doubt their pursuers were following the same path they'd just traversed.

Colt raced up two floors of the parking structure, then headed for the last aisle, backed into the very last spot and turned the engine off. "Everybody out. We have to find a new ride before they get to this floor."

"The fourth floor has a car rental parking lot. We can snag a vehicle there." Maren's door wouldn't open because he'd hugged up against the wall. Grabbing her backpack, she and the dogs scooted across the driver's seat and out the driver's-side door, squeezing between the truck and a compact sedan.

Colt leashed Rusk and kept him close while Maren clipped Haven's lead to her collar.

Keeping to a crouch, they hustled to the staircase and went up to the fourth floor.

When they came out onto the level where the car rental agency had a fleet of minivans, SUVs and sedans, she searched for the lot attendant. She spotted him wiping down a minivan. She gestured to Colt. "There."

They hustled to the attendant, showed the twentysomething-year-old guy their badges. "We need to commandeer a vehicle. Something big enough for the dogs. Hurry."

He led them to a metal box with multiple keys dangling from hooks. He grabbed a set and handed them over. "The gray SUV. You'll explain to my boss, right?"

"Yep," Colt said. "I'll make sure you're in the clear for this."

The young man stuck his hands in his pocket and watched them run to the SUV.

Colt undid all the locks on the door. With little coaxing, the dogs jumped into the back passenger seat.

Maren opted to let Colt continue to drive and settled in the front passenger seat while he climbed into the driver's seat.

Headlights coming up the ramp at a fast clip had her heart rate spiking.

"Down!" Colt yelled.

"Down!" Maren repeated.

Both dogs hunched on the floorboard of the back seat. Maren slid down until she was out of view. Colt launched himself sideways so that they were practically cheek to cheek. His nearness sent unexpected awareness fluttering through her. She held herself still as they waited, their breaths mingling.

The slow-moving black truck went past. She didn't breathe until it rounded the curve and went up to the top floor.

Colt eased upright to look out the window.

"It won't take them long to come back this way." Colt hit the emergency onboard service system button on the SUV's rearview mirror.

A disembodied, female voice spoke through the speakers. "This is Start Assist, my name is Helen," the voice said. "Are you having car trouble?"

"This is DEA Agent Colt Dawson," Colt said and rattled off his badge number.

"And this is Officer Maren Anderson," Maren said and spoke her badge number. "We're being chased. Our lives are being threatened."

"I will dispatch officers to your location," Helen offered.

"Thank you, Helen," Colt said. He told her the license plate of the black truck and signed off.

Hopefully, the local police would stop the truck, which would give them time to get farther away.

Colt started the vehicle, shifted into Reverse, and backed the SUV out of the parking space. Slowly, he drove out of the parking structure.

Maren kept low as the "borrowed" SUV hummed along the highway. Adrenaline ebbed and fatigue pulled at her as the late afternoon sun sparked off the hood. She could hardly believe it had been only that morning she'd left her house before dawn to travel to Barren Valley. So much had happened.

Her sister was alive and in danger.

It was up to Maren and Colt to save her.

She turned toward her new partner. "Let's lose these guys and go find Vinnie Homer."

Then she lifted up a prayer that the man would have the information they needed.

SEVEN

Colt managed to evade their pursuers by slipping into city traffic undetected. He kept an eye on the rearview mirror as he wove through the throng of cars, and they remained clear as they left town. Now he drove slowly toward where Pine Creek flowed under the I-25 interstate near Woodman Avenue. A large encampment had been constructed with tents and makeshift shelters of plywood and boxes.

Sadness invaded his chest. He knew many of these people had no other choice than to live on public property. For some it was a lifestyle of their own design. But many had issues that the system couldn't deal with. The unhoused situation was one the whole country had yet to solve. Colt had no answers either. The only way he could help was by stopping the drug supply chain. Which meant bringing down Shadow.

He parked several blocks away from the encampment, tucking the SUV behind a building with the hope that no one would mess with the vehicle while they were gone.

It was by the grace of God that they had managed to evade the men in the black 4x4 truck that had chased them into the parking garage. Just because the men on the street hadn't had weapons at that time didn't mean by the time they got into their vehicle and followed them they hadn't armed themselves.

And telling Maren about his cousin and the young boy he hadn't been able to save left him feeling drained. He'd known it was the right thing to do since he knew her story, but sharing didn't come easy.

And now an awkwardness rested between them as they leashed up the dogs and headed down the street to the houseless encampment.

Armed with a photo of Vinnie Homer on their phones, they split up, showing the photo to anyone who would talk to them. An hour later, they were no closer to finding Vinnie.

Frustrated and fatigued as the sun began to set, he sent up a prayer asking God for help, for some sign or direction. Anything that would lead them to Vinnie, who could lead them to Opal and ultimately to Shadow.

His phone rang.

Maren.

Pushing the talk button, he said, "Everything okay?"

"I found someone who might know where Vinnie went." Her voice vibrated with anticipation. "I'm at the far end of the encampment."

"On our way." He hung up and handed some cash to the old woman who was petting Rusk.

"Bless you," the woman said, tucking the money into the pocket of her pants.

With anticipation making his and Rusk's stride hurried, Colt sent up a quick prayer, asking God to lead them in the right direction so they could find Opal before it was too late.

It didn't take long to find Maren talking to an older man missing several teeth. His grizzled face, graying hair and tattered clothes suggested he'd been on the street for a long time. In his hand, he held several bills. Colt didn't have to ask to know that Maren had provided the cash.

"Colt, this is Mortimer, he's a veteran," Maren said gently. "Mortimer thinks he might know where Vinnie went."

Mortimer pocketed the money and then held out his hand to Colt.

Understanding, Colt dug into his pocket and pulled out his wallet. He only had a twenty left. He handed it over. "Mr. Mortimer, can you tell us where Vinnie is?"

"Just Mortimer. And not exactly," Mortimer said.

Maren made a distressed noise in her throat.

Colt put a hand on her arm, calming her. "What can you tell us?"

Mortimer shrugged. "He went with the lady, the one from the mission."

That was something at least. "Do you remember her name? Or the name of the mission?"

"Gospel something." Mortimer turned around and darted back into his tent.

"Really? That's it?" Maren's upset was apparent. "Not much to go on."

"Just wait," Colt said. He'd dealt with many homeless people over the years and knew patience was the key. Mortimer would tell them what he knew in his own time.

Mortimer emerged from his tent and triumphantly held up a flyer. "Here you go. That's where he is. Or at least that's who he left with. People from there."

Maren snatched the flyer from him and looked it over. "I know where this is."

"Thank you, Mortimer." Colt shook the man's hand.

"Yes, we appreciate this info," Maren added.

By the time they got back to the SUV, it was well past eight in the evening.

"The mission will be closed for the night," she said. "But we could still go there."

"Not a good idea," he countered. "Waiting for daylight, when Vinnie will be more at ease, is the right call."

She considered, then said, "We can't go back to your camper. I'm sure they probably have someone watching it. We can go to my place."

Worry had Colt saying, "We don't know if your home has been compromised."

"If anyone in Shadow's organization knew about me, we'd know," she said. "Besides, it isn't in my name."

"No?" Colt found that curious since she professed not to date. Not that her marital status meant anything to him.

"The townhome belonged to my uncle," she explained. "He took guardianship of Opal and me after our parents died. He passed when we were twenty-one. I never officially changed the name on the deed even though I continued living there."

He could insist they stay at a hotel, but since neither of them had supplies with them for themselves or the dogs, her place made sense. And he could protect her if Shadow's men did find her. "All right." He wished he'd thought to grab his go bag out of the back compartment of his truck. "Is there a superstore on the way we can stop at and get a few things?"

"As a matter of fact, there's one down the street from my place," she said. "We'll stop on the way."

"Sounds like a brilliant plan."

The stop at the store took less than fifteen minutes as he gathered a few clothing items and toiletries.

When he got back into the SUV, she gave him directions to a set of row houses near the University of Colorado. She hopped out at the back entrance gate and punched in a number on the keypad. A moment later, the large metal gate rolled up.

When she got back into the vehicle, she said, "Pull into spot 304."

Once they were parked and had the dogs leashed up, he followed her to the front door of her three-story townhome.

She stepped aside so he could enter then shut and locked the door behind him.

His gaze roamed over the first floor of the three-story townhome. Bright-colored throw pillows mingled with soft leather. The walls were painted a soft green. The living and kitchen space were an eclectic mix of practical and whimsy. He wondered which was she? The more practical or the whimsy?

An awkward silence descended. He broke the tension by asking, "Do you mind if I clean up?"

Her eyes flared and she gestured toward a hallway. "Of course. The guest bath is the last door on the right on this floor," she said. "I always keep fresh towels hanging. There's everything you should need in there." She moved to the kitchen counter. "You think Rusk would eat Haven's food? Or can I scramble him an egg?"

"He'll eat most anything." He appreciated her thoughtful care of Rusk. And her thoughtfulness toward him. It had been a long time since someone other than family showed him such consideration. Rebecca hadn't been the nurturing type.

Maren filled two bowls with dry food and set them on a rubber mat in the kitchen.

"Make yourself at home," she told him. "My bedroom is on the top floor. The middle floor is a bonus room and an office. The guest room is across the hall from the guest bath."

"Was the bedroom and bath on this floor your uncle's?"

The frosted overhead lights lit her blue eyes. "It was. Though I changed everything out." She smiled. "His style was a throwback to his youth in the sixties. Over the years, I've pretty much changed the whole place, since I had it to myself when Opal left."

He noted the subtle sadness in her tone. "It must be lonely living here by yourself."

She made a face as if regretting the slip in emotion. "I have Haven. I don't need anyone else."

He could relate to the sentiment. "Which is why you don't date."

Inclining her head, she said, "Exactly."

It seemed they were cut from the same cloth. Two individuals determined to stay unattached and unencumbered by emotions.

For some reason, as he left her and made his way down the hall, the thought left him feeling unsettled.

While Colt freshened up, Maren did the same. She showered and changed into comfy, wide-leg, stretchy pants and a long tunic sweater that dropped off one shoulder. Her hair fell in waves over her back. It felt good to let the strands stay loose rather than in the braid or bun that she wore normally when working.

To keep herself busy as well as stave off the worry for her twin and distract herself from the fact a man was in her home, Maren prepared a dinner of spaghetti and meatballs. Thankfully, the bagged salad she'd bought before she'd left for Barren Valley was still good. It felt odd to be making dinner for two. For so long, she'd been alone.

But content. At least, that was the story she told herself, and if she repeated it often enough, it would be true. Telling Colt she was fine on her own wasn't a lie. She just couldn't admit that there were times she yearned for more. But more came with heartache that she wouldn't accept.

She'd always prided herself on being okay with being alone. She'd convinced herself she preferred her life without any entanglements. Sure, she missed her sister, but she never really contemplated what it would be like to have someone to care for, to cook for, to love.

She couldn't stop the little tremor of anticipation, the flicker of hope, that Colt would enjoy the meal. Even as the thought formed, she shut it down.

This wasn't a date. This was two professionals who needed sustenance and rest before continuing their quest to find Opal and, ultimately, Shadow. Because as long as Shadow was allowed to operate, she and her sister were in danger.

And hopefully, Shadow would have intel on the baby smuggling ring that could help them find Mia Andrews.

When Colt emerged from the bathroom smelling of the apple shampoo she'd bought on a whim to put in the guest shower, her heart did a little thump. The scent would forever remind her of him.

His dark chestnut hair was damp and curling at the ends. He'd trimmed his facial hair and changed into a long-sleeve, soft-looking chambray shirt and a pair of black cargo pants.

He wore bright white socks and no shoes. For some reason, the sight had a strange impact on her, as if him being shoeless was somehow very personal and intimate. The sleeves of the chambray shirt were rolled up to his elbows, showing off his corded forearms, which also affected her in ways she wasn't used to. For a fleeting moment, she imagined what life would be like with a man like him. A man who gave as good as he got, a man with honor and integrity.

Rusk jumped up from his resting spot near the couch to inspect his handler. It was enough of a distraction for her to pull her attention away from Colt.

"Yum, something smells delicious," he said as he parked himself at the end of the counter, his big body taking up space in the kitchen, though she didn't feel crowded at all. His presence was comfortable and exhilarating at the same time.

And she really needed to get a grip.

"Don't get too excited," she quipped, busying herself by wiping down the counter. "Sauce from a jar, frozen meatballs, premade salad, and thankfully some sliced sourdough made into garlic bread."

"Maren, I am grateful," he said. "This is the closest I've come to a home-cooked meal in a very long time."

She remembered his description of his family. "Now, I know that's not true. I'm sure you go to your parents' quite often for a home-cooked meal."

He held up his hands. "True. But not the same thing. Having

your mother cook for you as opposed to an unrelated, beautiful woman—" He shook his head. "Not the same thing at all."

He thought she was beautiful.

Heat infused her cheeks and a thrill raced down her spine at his implication that there was more to this meal, to their time together, than professional partnership.

Ridiculous.

Turning away, she took the seasoned sourdough slices out of the oven and slid them onto a large platter. Picking up the platter, she handed it to him. "Did you find everything you needed at the store?"

He put his hands on the platter, but didn't immediately take it from her. His gaze searched her face. She held steady, not about to let on how he affected her, yet she couldn't deny the zing of attraction arcing between them.

He gave a gentle tug on the platter. "I did, thank you."

Releasing her hold, she turned away and resisted the urge to fan herself. Why did she feel flushed?

Briskly, she served up two plates of spaghetti and carried them to the table where she'd arranged two place settings across from each other. No sitting side by side. That would be too weird. Too intimate.

"I have to say your place isn't quite what I expected." He lifted the pitcher of water and filled both their glasses.

She brought over the salad bowl and two smaller plates.

Taking her seat, she said, "I'm almost afraid to ask, but what did you expect?"

He held her gaze. "Functional. With no personality."

Her defenses rose and she tucked in her chin, her eyebrows rising so high she probably thought they blended in with her hairline. "Excuse me?"

The sides of his mouth lifted in a teasing smile. "Seriously. I expected the practical, but I didn't expect the whimsy. When you're on the job, there's very little whimsy evident."

Mulling over his words, she dished out the salad. There had been a time in her life when she'd been much more whimsical. Before her parents' deaths. Before Opal became addicted to drugs. Before her uncle died. While the repeated blows had tried to knock her down, she was still fighting to stand tall. "A girl's got to have a little mystery."

His low chuckle pleased her. Way more than it should. Time to change the subject. "Tell me more about your family."

One of his chestnut eyebrows lifted.

She had the feeling he knew exactly what she was doing. As long as he was talking, she didn't have to. Giving him a specific topic would keep the focus off the troubling plight of her sister. And off Maren. She didn't like being the focus of attention. Plus, she liked hearing about his big family. So different from hers.

For the next hour, while they ate, he regaled her with childhood exploits of his and his siblings.

"It all sounds so wonderful and too good to be true." But he was the living proof that some families were healthy and functional. Unlike hers.

"Even before our parents were killed," she admitted, "I remember the stilted dinners with the four of us. The quiet evenings spent reading, or listening to my mother rehearse her lectures while our dad was engrossed in his research."

"Both of your parents were academics?"

"They were," she said. "My father was a professor of theology, and my mother taught social sciences." A path neither she nor Opal had followed.

"I'm so sorry you lost them."

"They weren't lost. They were killed," she said, an edge to her voice she couldn't contain. "Most likely by somebody driving drunk. And I will never have closure."

The sympathy in his eyes had her heart quaking.

"Probably not in this lifetime." He slid his hand across the table and folded his fingers over her clenched fist. "Faith in

Jesus is about trusting that what happens here on earth will be reconciled in Heaven."

She'd heard similar sentiments from her pastor and others over the years. It didn't diminish the loss or even the hurt. But for some reason, in this moment, the words did offer comfort. Or did the balm come from Colt himself? There was something reassuring about him, about his steadfast belief.

She stared at where their hands met. What would it be like to have someone in her life who knew her? Whom she could fully trust? Someone she was willing to risk letting into her heart?

Talk about a pipe dream.

Even if there was some sort of future where she and Colt might explore the currents of attraction running circles around them, they both had very precarious jobs that put them in the line of fire. She couldn't go through another loss.

Unaccountably sad, she slipped her hand away and began clearing the table, aware of his inscrutable gaze. He moved to help, which only endeared him to her more, and they worked in companionable silence.

When the dishes were done and the kitchen back in order, she said, "We should take the dogs out back."

She led the way to the back door and opened it wide. Haven jumped up from her bed under the front window and raced outside. Rusk was right after her. She and Colt stepped out onto the small back porch. The grassy area was enclosed with a white picket fence. It was the closest she would ever get to that sort of life. A thought that usually didn't bother her. Tonight, strangely, it did. Why was that?

As she and Colt stood side by side in the dark, watching over the dogs, she gave voice to a question that plagued her mind. "Do you ever doubt God?"

"Yes," he admitted softly. "Faith is not a destination, it's a journey. Every day, I have to be intentional about releasing what I can't control."

She let his words wrap around her, seeping into the bruised places of her heart.

"Intentional," she said, rolling the word around in her brain. "I like that. Sometimes I'm selfish. I forget that there's more to this life than just me or the circumstances I find myself in."

"Somehow, I doubt you could ever be selfish," he said. "You wouldn't be as good at your job if you didn't care about others. If you didn't work toward the greater good. Don't sell yourself short."

His arms slid around her shoulders, and she stiffened. He turned her to face him. The moon's glow didn't reveal more than the planes of his face, the shape of his mouth, in the dark. But she watched his lips move as he said, "You're a good person, Maren Anderson. Don't ever lose hope."

Sudden tears pricked her eyes. She could feel herself leaning toward him. Her breath caught. What was happening?

A deep yearning to kiss him welled inside her chest.

Alarm bells went off in her head.

No, no, no.

It was all the frantic adrenaline of the last seventeen hours. She was getting caught up in the moment. She was finding herself attracted, not only physically but also emotionally, to this man. She couldn't allow it. Too much was at stake.

Her sister. The mission to take down a dangerous drug kingpin. The urgency to stop an illegal adoption ring preying on young moms-to-be.

Her heart.

Allowing something to happen between her and Colt would compromise their judgment. Even a simple kiss would be too much.

She turned away and whistled, drawing Haven immediately to her side. Rusk raced forward to sit beside his partner.

"We need to get some sleep," she said briskly. "Six a.m. will come pretty quickly. We'll need to make a quick stop at the task force headquarters to check out an official vehicle before we go to the mission."

Slowly, he released her and stepped back. His voice was just as curt. "Rusk and I will be ready."

EIGHT

The next morning, after toast and a cup of coffee, Maren felt more in control of her emotions. Though she'd been up and ready before six, because she'd had a horrible night's sleep. Her brain would not turn off. She'd tossed and turned with her mind whirling with thoughts of Opal and Shadow. And mostly of Colt.

She'd wanted to kiss him last night.

A lapse she could not afford.

She needed to stay focused. Keep her edge in case Shadow's men showed up.

After heading to the task force headquarters with Colt and the dogs, a drive that took nearly two hours in rush hour traffic, she arranged to use an unmarked Tahoe in exchange for their rental SUV. She'd elicited a promise from a fellow officer to return the vehicle to the rental agency with apologies.

Thankfully, the dogs shared the specialized compartment in the official SUV companionably.

Dev, the lead trainer for the task force, stopped by the motor pool just as they were about to head out. "I take it Haven and Rusk get along?"

Understanding his surprise that both dogs, who could be fierce in their own right, would tolerate the same enclosed space, she said, "If they were both male, or both female, it would be a different story."

"Too true," he said.

"How's the search for a new trainer going?" she asked.

"I have several candidates we're interviewing," Dev replied. "It's a hard decision."

She didn't envy him finding his replacement.

He gave her a wave and walked away. "Take care."

They left the task force building and made their way to the Gospel Mission Recovery Center on the far side of town. Once again, Maren was content to let Colt take the wheel. She had no problems with him in control of the vehicle. It gave her the opportunity to keep an eye out for danger while contemplating questions she wanted to ask Vinnie about Opal. If Vinnie was indeed at the shelter. She prayed he would be.

Colt parked the vehicle in the center's vast parking lot, and they released the dogs from the back compartment. They each leashed up their respective K-9 and kept them close as they approached the large, rectangular brick building.

Inside the lobby, they showed their badges and asked to speak with the woman who canvassed the houseless encampment near the highway underpass.

A few minutes later, a woman in her mid-fifties approached. "Hello, I understand you're looking for me?"

"Yes. I'm Officer Maren Anderson and this is DEA Agent Colt Dawson," Maren said. "And you are?"

"Cindy Gregson," she said. "I'm the director. How can I help?"

"You brought in a homeless man from the underpass camp," Colt said. "His name is Vinnie Homer. We'd like to speak with him."

Maren held her breath, hoping the man was still in residence.

"I wasn't aware that Vinnie was in trouble with the law," Cindy said, carefully.

"He was a witness to an apparent drowning," Colt said. "We have some follow-up questions."

Empathy crossed Cindy's features. "He told me about that

poor young woman." She gestured for them to follow her. "He was quite broken up. I think that's what finally allowed him to seek help. He's been sober for the last few months."

Cindy led them down the hallway, past several rooms with two sets of bunk beds lining both walls. She stopped at the doorway of a room at the far end and stayed in the hallway but called out, "Vinnie, may we enter?"

Maren exchanged an interested glance with Colt. Apparently, Cindy was showing respect for Vinnie and his roommate's space. Maren could appreciate that.

"Sure, come on in," a thin, nasal voice came from inside the room.

Maren filed into the small space behind Cindy. The room was tidy with only one of the bunk beds occupied. A pudgy man in his late twenties sat on the edge of the bottom bunk. He had blond, curly hair that shifted over his brow as he lifted his head. His eyes widened as he caught sight of Maren.

He stood up abruptly, bonking his head on the top bunk. He sat back down and rubbed his scalp. "What's happening here?"

"These officers have some questions for you regarding the girl who drowned," Cindy said, gently.

Vinnie's eyes met Maren's. "You shouldn't be here. What if he finds out? You're posing as a cop?"

Cindy's dark eyes grew round as she stared at Maren. "What is he talking about?"

Colt held up a hand. "It's all right. Vinnie is mistaken. This is Maren Anderson. Opal's sister."

Vinnie visibly deflated with a noisy exhale. "Right. She mentioned a sister. But she didn't say you look alike. I don't understand."

Maren's heart bumped. "She mentioned me?"

"She did. She said you were her only family, and she didn't want to drag you into her mess. She didn't trust that you wouldn't—" He clamped his lips together, cutting off the rest of his words.

Maren stepped forward and Haven kept pace.

Vinnie's eyes grew round as he noticed the dog. He scrambled back to the wall underneath the bunk. "Are you going to hurt me?"

Taking a breath to control her upset, Maren crouched down and gestured for Haven to lie on the floor next to her. "We are not here to hurt you. But I need you to tell me everything you know about my sister. I have to find her."

Vinnie shook his head. "She drowned. She's dead. Nobody can hurt her anymore."

Rage at the thought of someone hurting her sister thrummed through her blood. "Who would hurt her?"

Vinnie shook his head. "He'll hurt me, too."

"Are you talking about Shadow?" Colt crouched down next to Maren and peered at Vinnie. Rusk sat with his gaze trained on the man pressed against the wall.

"He's got eyes and ears everywhere," Vinnie said, his gaze going to Cindy.

Colt stood and cupped Cindy by the elbow. "Thank you for your help. But we have it from here. You may go."

Cindy hesitated. "I'm not sure—"

"Out," Maren practically growled, her impatience growing exponentially. Haven responded to the growl in Maren's voice by scrambling to her feet.

"I'll be just down the hall if you need me, Vinnie," Cindy said before hurrying out of the room.

Colt shut the door behind her.

Keeping her voice as even as possible, Maren said to Vinnie, "We know my sister faked her death to get out from under Shadow's thumb. Do you know where she would go?"

Blinking rapidly, Vinnie shook his head. "I don't. She told me it was better if I didn't know."

Frustration pounded against Maren's temples. "Do you know how to get a hold of her?"

Vinnie licked his lips but didn't answer. Hope rose within Maren. His hesitation had to mean he actually did know how to get a hold of her sister. Purposefully, gentling her voice even more, she coaxed, "Please, I need to find her before Shadow does. There are bad men out there looking for her. They will kill her. And her baby."

"A baby? I didn't know." A tear rolled down Vinnie's cheek. "I can get her a message. I don't know if she'll respond."

"You need to tell her that Maren is looking for her and that we can get her in a safe house," Colt said.

Vinnie slowly eased out from under the upper bunk bed and stood. There was a small desk wedged between the wall and the end of the bunk bed. From the drawer he pulled out a burner phone. "I'll text her. If she responds, I'll let you know." He clutched the phone to his chest. "That's the best I can do for you. My loyalty is to Opal and Georgy." His face fell. "Georgy is gone now. Oh man, I need a hit."

Maren's heart ached for the man and his struggles with addiction. Seeing Vinnie so distraught and craving drugs brought back memories of Opal and her dependence on the poison she'd relied on to numb her emotions. Maren reached for a tissue from the box on the bedside table and then withdrew her business card from her pocket. She handed both to Vinnie. "Contact me at this number. You can also give it to Opal. She might prefer to reach out to me directly. Or maybe not."

Pain twisted in her chest. Her sister had always known how to reach her.

Vinnie nodded as he took the card and the tissue. He used the tissue to wipe at his runny nose as he stared at her card as if mesmerized by the rectangular paper.

"You don't need a hit," Colt said to him. "You're stronger than you believe. You're here—that means you want to get help.

There's got to be a group, or therapist, you can talk to right now. Don't blow this chance at recovery."

Doubts swirled in Vinnie's bloodshot eyes as they lifted. "I want to get better."

"You will." Colt's voice held a note of certainty. "You just have to push through the hard parts."

"The hard parts," Vinnie repeated as if it were a mantra.

Before leaving, Colt asked, "Have you ever seen Shadow face-to-face?"

Vinnie shook his head. "Naw. Opal has, though."

The information sent a ribbon of dread slicing through Maren, confirming why Shadow wanted her sister dead. She could identify him.

"That would definitely motivate Shadow to want her gone before she talks to the authorities," Colt said.

"We have to find her before he does." But where would her sister go?

"Please save her," Vinnie whispered.

With her heart in her throat, Maren left with Colt, the dogs close at their heels. Once they were in the Tahoe and driving away, Maren said, "I want to see where Opal went into the water. Maybe the investigators missed something. Maybe I missed something." Maybe her sister would return to the river. "And the dogs could use a bit of free time." She considered and then added, "I need some fresh air as well."

Just a few moments to regroup and reassess her next moves.

Colt nodded. "It's worth a shot."

Colt drove out of town toward the Arkansas River. The city falling away to reveal more rugged landscape. He found the dirt road leading to the spot along the river where Opal had supposedly gone in. His heart hurt for Maren. It must've been hard to hear that her sister hadn't wanted to contact her or ask her for help. It didn't make sense. But he'd learned long ago that life rarely went as expected or hoped.

Even though he knew the dogs needed the downtime, as well as he and Maren, the river always made him nervous. It was rough and wild. The rapids sweeping down the rocky bottom were a sight to behold. A dangerous sight. Anyone going into the water without lifesaving protection was asking for trouble. And even then, serious injury was more common than not.

From the moment he'd heard that Opal had gone into the water and not resurfaced, his stomach had been twisted in knots.

He knew the damage the river could cause. He'd once worked a case where drug smugglers were using the rapids to move their product. When one of their rafts had flipped, the two occupants didn't survive. Their bodies, battered and busted, had been found miles downstream.

He supposed that was one of the reasons he hadn't bought that Opal had died in the river. Her body had never been found. Authorities had searched these riverbanks. But now that he knew it was all a hoax, he gritted his teeth against the frustration of law enforcement wasting so much time. Bringing the SUV to a halt at the end of a long dirt road, he climbed out with Maren and they released the dogs.

"There doesn't seem to be anyone around," Maren said. "I'm leaving Haven unleashed to let her just be a dog for a bit."

Nodding, Colt stuffed Rusk's leash into one of the pockets of his new cargo pants. "Will Haven know to stay out of the water?"

"She might venture to the edge," Maren said. "But I'll bring her back before she can go much farther."

"These rapids are no joke," he said. "Rusk knows the rules."

Maren stared off into the distance at the rising Rocky Mountains. "Do you think Vinnie will reach my sister?"

Colt followed her gaze, taking in the rugged landscape, the distinct peaks and valleys that made up the mountain range.

"I pray so," he said. "For your sake, as well as for the investigation."

She slanted him a glance. "I appreciate that."

His phone buzzed. Looking at the caller ID, he hesitated.

"Who is it?" Concern laced her words. "Vinnie?"

Quick to reassure her, he said, "Just my mom. I'll call her back."

Maren blew out a breath. There was no need for her to say she was disappointed it wasn't news of her sister.

"No, you should answer," she said. "It's family. Family's important. You never know when you'll have another chance."

Gut twisting at the dire truth in her words, he nodded. "I'll be just a moment."

He strode away from Maren and the sound of the water crashing over the rocky riverbed. Rusk, seeing his handler moving, hurried to his side.

"Mom? Is everything okay?" he asked while plugging one ear to hear.

"Of course, dear." His mother's voice filled his head. "I'm calling to remind you of your nieces' birthday party tomorrow."

"Oh, right." He had forgotten. "I'll make it if I can."

"That's all I ask," she said. Then she went on about preparations for the party—

"Mom, Mom," he interrupted her. "I'm in the middle of a case. I have to go."

"I understand, dear," she said. "Remember we love you."

"I know, Mom. Thanks." He hung up. He loved his big, boisterous family. The thought of losing any of them made him queasy. How did Maren function knowing her sister was in danger?

Putting the phone back in his pocket, Colt lifted his eyes to the bright blue sky and watched an airplane darting across, leaving a white trail in its wake. "Okay, Lord, please give us a break in this case. Show us how to find Opal."

A shout and Haven's fierce barking shuddered through Colt. Rusk sprinted away, ahead of Colt. He ran back toward the riverbed.

His heart stuttered at the sight of Maren being dragged toward the river by two masked men.

NINE

Maren struggled against her captors. She'd had no time to mount a real defense before the two masked men had crept out of the dense spread of juniper bushes, like apparitions, and had grabbed hold of her arms. The pair attempted to drag her toward the rushing water of the Arkansas River. She dug in her heels.

"Boss wants you dead," one of the assailants ground out. "There's a hefty bonus for anyone who makes you disappear."

His words slammed into her with enough force to suck the breath from her lungs. Once again, she was being mistaken for Opal. How had these two found her? Had they been staking out the area?

Their intent was clear. They wanted to drown her. Her feet tried to find purchase in the loose rocks of the riverbed. They pushed her forward, forcing her to splash into the river. The icy cold mountain water had her sucking in a sharp breath. She stumbled over the rocks. One of the assailants grabbed a handful of her hair and tried to force her face-first into the rushing rapids.

"Haven!" she shouted. The dog had disappeared while exploring. "Attack!"

Within seconds, a streak of red and brown came into view. The dog easily leaped over rocks and a fallen log to get to her handler. She snarled and barked as she raced to help Maren.

One of the men swore, released his hold on her arm before running away.

The remaining masked assailant tightened his grip on Maren's hair and arm but remained frozen as if debating what to do.

Taking advantage of having an arm free, she pummeled her attacker with her fist, punching him in the face and using her elbow to clock him in the side of the head. He continued to hang on to her arm though he released her hair. His fingers dug painfully into her biceps through her clothes.

Haven lunged, biting into the meaty part of the attacker's calf, her teeth sinking into flesh, drawing blood.

The man screamed, a bloodcurdling sound that echoed across the valley, mingling with the roar of the white water rapids.

She heard another scream, but didn't dare remove her attention from the masked assailant who still refused to release his iron grip. He was tenacious.

But so was she.

A well-placed knee in the groin sent the man doubling over and he finally let go of her arm. Haven shook her head, causing the man to lose his balance, and he went to the ground, splashing into the water.

Backing up and drawing her weapon, Maren gave the release command, "Out."

Haven released her bite on the man's calf, backed up but stayed in front of Maren and snarled, baring her teeth, threatening to bite the man again.

Noise behind Maren had her spinning with the gun aimed at whatever threat was coming toward her.

Colt marched forward, escorting the runaway assailant with his hands cuffed behind his back, and Rusk nipping at the man's heels. Glad to see her partner had captured the guy, she lowered the barrel of her weapon.

Turning back to the man groaning on the ground and clutching his calf while blood seeped through his fingers, Maren said, "You're under arrest. Hands behind your back."

"You gotta get me help," the guy said, his voice filled with pain. "I'm gonna bleed out."

"Unlikely," she said. "It's just your calf. Nothing vital there."

She holstered her gun, grasped the man, dragged him out of the water onto dry soil and flipped him onto his stomach. Yanking his hands behind his back, she pulled a zip tie from her pocket and slipped it over his wrists and cinched it tight. Taking off her blazer, she ripped the sleeve of her blouse and wrapped it around the man's calf.

Even though there were no major blood vessels to worry about, she didn't want dirt to get into the wound and become infected. Then she ripped the mask off the man. She'd never seen the dark-haired guy before. He had a wide nose, dark eyes and pockmarks on his cheeks.

"I've already called for backup." Colt pushed the other assailant to his knees. "I saw you had that one handled, figured I'd keep this one from getting away."

"I appreciate it," she said.

"Are you okay?" Concern deepened his voice.

"Dandy." She gestured to the assailants. "They said their boss wanted me dead."

Understanding lit Colt's eyes. "Ah." He peeled the mask off the man he'd cuffed. He too was a stranger. "Your boss is Shadow?"

The man sneered but didn't say anything.

Colt huffed out a noisy breath. "I'll take that as a yes. How did you know we were here?"

Though neither man answered, Maren noticed the way they both glanced toward the dense clump of bushes from where they'd come out. She stalked over and pushed aside the tangled branches of the juniper to discover a cell phone. She hoped it would have a way to track Shadow. Donning latex gloves, she slipped the phone into her pocket. Then she marched back to the assailants.

"Things will go a lot better for you to if you tell us where Shadow is," Maren told the two men.

Both men made faces and stayed silent.

Sirens rent the air.

Maren crouched down and grabbed the face of the man Haven had bitten. "Tell me where to find Shadow."

"I want a lawyer," the man ground out.

Maren released him and stood, fisting her hands at her sides.

"We won't get anything out of them," Colt said. "They're more afraid of Shadow than they are of the police."

"Because Shadow has people in the police departments." Maren's insides twisted. "And now they'll let Shadow or someone who will relay a message to Shadow know that you're DEA and I'm a cop."

"Couldn't be helped," he replied. "Though I'm sure Shadow knows who I am since I've been trying to bring him down for over a year."

Several police cruisers ground to a halt near their vehicle.

Maren recognized many of the officers. She hated to think that one of them was dirty. "Can you deal with them while I call Emmett?"

"Of course." Colt strode away to talk to the local police.

Maren contacted the task force leader. She quickly updated him on this latest attempt on her life and being mistaken for Opal again. "We're still no closer to discovering Shadow's location. But I did find a cell phone. I'll get it to Eva as soon as we can."

"You'll catch a break," Emmett said. "I feel it in my bones."

"Thanks, boss," she said, hoping his words were true. "We need to bring Vinnie Homer into protective custody."

"I'll contact the US Marshals Service and have them take Mr. Homer into protective custody. And let Colt know I'll update

Special Agent in Charge Herman." Emmett referred to Colt's direct boss at the DEA.

"Will do." Maren prayed the marshals would be able to keep Vinnie Homer safe. The man had falsely reported Opal's death. But he was the only link to finding her sister.

After giving her statement to the local police, she watched as the two men were put into the back of a cruiser. They would be taken to the county jail, where they would be formally charged and arraigned.

Once she and Colt were alone again, she said, "Emmett's going to relay an update to your boss."

"I was about to do that," Colt said. "Good to know."

Blowing out a breath, she asked, "How did Shadow know to send men here?"

For a moment, Colt didn't respond, but she could see he was thinking. Then his eyes widened, and he reached into his pocket for his phone. He held it up. "Somehow, they've been tracking me. Maybe malware or an app I'm not aware of. That's how they knew to find Opal at the clinic. They know I'm trying to find her. Could be how they found out about our visit to Steve and how they found us here." He powered down the phone.

"We can have Eva go through both of our phones along with the burner phone and see what she can find out," Maren said. "My boss said he'd contact the US Marshals to pick up Vinnie."

"We can't go back to your house," Colt said.

"If Shadow knew about my place, why didn't he send men last night?"

"Don't know," he said. "But we can't assume he doesn't send them now. Maybe he was waiting to see where we would go."

Frustration crimped her chest. They may have led the drug kingpin straight to Vinnie. She sent up a silent prayer that the marshals would get to Vinnie before Shadow did.

She met Colt's gaze, saw the worry there. "We have to go back to my place, at least long enough to grab some things.

I'll let Emmett know we need backup. I think it would be wise to have a task force member we know we can trust to provide extra protection in case we're tailed to a hotel."

"Fair enough," he said.

They left the river area and met Colorado K-9 Unit member Officer Lizzie Reynolds and her golden retriever, a spectacular tracking dog named Reena, at the front door of the town house.

"I appreciate you coming," Maren said to the petite blonde.

Though Haven and Reena had been around each other a few times the past few months, Maren kept Haven close.

The two female dogs eyed each other but neither showed any sign of aggression toward the other.

"Of course," Lizzie replied, as her curious, green-eyed gaze took in Colt and Rusk. The pointer cocked his head to study Reena and her K-9 handler. "Glad to help."

Maren made the introduction. Colt and Lizzie shook hands.

"I'd heard we had DEA on board," Lizzie stated. "Nice to meet you."

"Likewise." Colt's voice was polite, but his gaze moved up and down the street. "We should hurry."

With Lizzie and Reena staying on guard out front, Maren and Colt, with their dogs, hustled inside.

Maren found an extra duffel bag for Colt to put the things he'd bought the night before into, while she packed a small suitcase. Then she bagged up Haven's food, treats and bowls.

After locking up the town house, she and Colt waved good-bye to Lizzie and then climbed back into the SUV.

"Let's head to Denver," Colt said. "We can find a dog-friendly hotel with connecting rooms and figure out our next move."

Worry churned in her gut. "I just hope Opal's in a safe place."

When would her sister reach out? Would she reach out?

Or would Shadow get to her before they could find her?

She couldn't go through the pain of losing her sister all over again.

Hopefully, whatever next move was decided on wouldn't lead to Opal being the one to mourn.

When they arrived at the hotel, part of a popular national chain, they secured adjoining rooms on the fifth floor. Even though the hotel normally didn't allow animals, the manager made an exception because Haven and Rusk were working dogs. Colt convinced Maren they needed to lie low for a bit, especially because he could tell she was shaken by the attack at the river. She'd agreed on the condition they buy a laptop and use their police access codes to run background checks on the men they'd apprehended and anyone else connected to Shadow and Opal.

Thankfully, there was an electronics store not far from the hotel. He bought a laptop and burner phones.

For most of the evening, they tried working different angles to the case. Maren put together a list of friends, associates and places she could remember Opal ever mentioning when they were still in touch with each other. They hoped something would provide a clue as to where she could be. But so far, nothing surfaced.

They even reached back out to Dr. Newton at the Barren Valley Clinic to see if Anna Parker had ever returned. But according to the doctor and the receptionist, Fran, the woman going by that name had never come back.

It was a fruitless endeavor and didn't make for a good night's sleep. At least for Colt. He tossed and turned. As soon as daylight hit, he was up and ready to start their investigation again. His first order of business was to call his SAC, Leo Herman.

"Colt here." He adjusted the phone and strode toward the hotel door. He wondered if Maren was up and dressed. He'd heard her moving around behind the closed door separating their rooms.

"Dawson, you had an exciting few days," Leo said. "I've been in contact with Special Agent Dane. Unfortunately, the men you arrested yesterday made bail late last night."

"What?" The hairs on Colt's nape rose at the distressing news. "That fast?"

"A slick lawyer arrived just before midnight, posted their bail and whisked them away," Leo's voice held a note of contempt. "Emmett and I tried to delay but Judge O'Hara signed off."

Colt gritted his teeth. The men were free. Colt only hoped they skipped town rather than facing Shadow and telling him they'd failed at their mission. Not willing to raise his suspicions that there was someone dirty within the DEA, Colt signed off.

There was a knock at the adjoining door. He opened it to find Maren dressed in black slacks, a cream-colored blouse, and a gray jacket, all of which hid the Kevlar vest beneath. She'd pulled her long, honey brown hair back into a low pony at her nape. Beside her, Haven sat, her dark eyes steady. Both looked ready to get to work. "Any word on Opal?"

Colt shook his head. He disliked seeing the look of disappointment in her eyes. He told her about the two men making bail.

"Ugh," she said. The one word held a world of frustration and anger. "We should call Emmett."

She used the burner phone and dialed the task force leader's number. Putting the call on speaker, Maren expressed her upset that the two assailants had been released.

Emmett confirmed the information given by Leo.

"Any chance the judge is dirty?" Colt asked.

"Anything is possible," Emmett replied. "I'll have our tech do a deep dive into his finances."

"Vinnie Homer?" Maren asked.

"US Marshals have him," Emmett said. "The marshals have

been instructed to contact you should Opal respond to Vinnie's message."

The wait was excruciating. He could only imagine how Maren was feeling.

"I could use both of you to provide support for Eli," Emmett told them. "We have another lead on the doctor Maren was tracking."

Checking his frustration, Colt said, "Give us the details."

Colt could see the conflicted emotions raging across Maren's face as they hung up from the call with Emmett. Colt understood the struggle; she wanted to pursue finding her sister but she also had a duty to the task force.

"Look, if our two cases are connected as we suspect, then focusing on the doctor right now just might lead us to Opal and Mia."

She heaved a sharp-sounding breath. "You're right." She rubbed her hands together. "Let's go get a dirty doctor."

As they headed out, he couldn't deny how much he liked her zeal. Who was he kidding? He liked her and could easily find himself longing for more than a professional relationship. The thought sent a fracture of worry through him. Becoming attached was the last thing he needed or wanted. His heart wasn't ready to take the risk.

But hunting down Shadow and the doctor who might be involved in the disappearance of Mia Andrews was more than enough danger for them all.

TEN

Maren stared at the free clinic in Buffalo Creek and couldn't help but remember the Barren Valley Clinic where she'd seen her sister. Somehow these two cases had to intersect. It just seemed too unlikely that her pregnant sister would show up at the Barren Valley Clinic where Dr. Derek Rolls once worked. But then again, it was possible that the whole thing was a coincidence. Opal was pregnant and the clinic was close to where she had been hiding out. Maybe Opal and Shadow weren't at all connected to the illegal baby adoption ring.

The knot in her stomach tightened. Worry bubbled up her throat, constricting the muscles.

Colt jumped from the SUV, pausing with the door open. "You coming?"

Shaking off her upset over her sister, Maren refocused her attention and took calming breaths. They were here to see if Dr. Rolls had once worked at this supposed clinic or if anyone knew how to find him. "Coming. Just getting a lay of the land."

She saw Eli Blackwood and Wrangler, his Belgian Malinois, step into view from beneath the shade of a tree.

Maren quickly climbed out of the SUV and circled around to the back to collect Haven. Rusk was already leashed and Colt was checking his phone.

Her heart bumped. "Any news?"

Tucking the phone back into his pocket, he said, "No, unfortunately." Trying not to let the disappointment show, Maren led Haven through the parking lot to where Eli, tall and intimidating, and his handsome K-9 with his dark-tipped ears and a muscled torso stood waiting.

She made the quick introduction.

"I don't know if this will pan out," Eli stated grimly. He was dressed in jeans and a Henley shirt with his badge on one hip and his sidearm on the other. "This doctor's a slippery one."

Maren agreed. "The best we can do is pray someone inside has information that's useful for the task force, and for finding Mia Andrews."

They filed into the clinic with Eli taking the lead. Maren and Haven came in next with Colt and Rusk bringing up the rear. They fanned out in the lobby. There were a few patients and spouses waiting in the blue plastic chairs.

Eli met her gaze and nodded toward the receptionist.

Taking his gesture as a sign she was to approach the front desk, she and Haven stepped forward to speak to the woman behind the counter.

"How can I help you today?" the receptionist said, her gaze bouncing between the three K-9 handlers and their dogs.

"I need to speak to the clinic director," she said. "It's regarding Dr. Derek Rolls."

"The director isn't in today," the receptionist said. "I'm Patty. I'm in charge for now. What questions can I answer?"

"Is Dr. Rolls employed here?"

Patty's face betrayed nothing. "He is not."

"Do you have a forwarding place of employment?"

Again, the woman's expression didn't so much as twitch. "We do not."

Maren couldn't ascertain if Patty even knew of whom she spoke. "Do you know Dr. Rolls?"

"We have no one here by that name," Patty stated firmly. "I'm sorry I couldn't be of help."

Was the woman being professional per legalities or was she in cahoots with the dirty doctor?

Eli stepped over. "He may be going by a different name. He's my height with short red hair and beard, and wears glasses."

"Silver-rimmed glasses," Maren supplied, remembering what Fran at the Barren Valley clinic had told her.

Patty shook her head. "Again, I'm sorry that description doesn't ring a bell."

"It does for me," a man, who'd been sitting quietly flipping through a magazine, spoke from his chair in the corner of the waiting room.

Maren, Eli and Colt turned toward him.

Colt was closest, so he stepped forward. "And you are?"

"Fred Harmony," the man said. He looked to be in his forties, with thick, salted hair and brown eyes. He wore chinos and a patterned, button-down shirt. "My wife is in being seen by the doctor."

Anticipation revving in her veins, Maren moved away from the reception counter to stand beside Colt. "Were you and your wife approached by Dr. Rolls?"

"Not us," Fred said. "My wife works at the community center here in town. There's a young girl who confided in Darcy that she was expecting. She told my wife a doctor had approached her saying he was in OB and could refer her to a low cost, maybe even free, clinic but he swore her to secrecy because he claimed they have little space and finances for more than one new patient."

Maren's gut clenched. Was this how the doctor lured his victims in? "This free clinic?" Maren asked, pointing at the floor.

"I don't think so," Fred replied. "Darcy would have said something if it was, right?"

"And she described the doctor?" Eli asked.

"She did. Darcy grew up here, so she'd asked thinking maybe

she'd recognize the doctor, but she didn't." Fred set aside the magazine in his hand. "Tall, red hair, beard and glasses."

"That's him." A blip of elation for being on the brink of learning something about the doctor had Maren's heart pumping in overdrive. "Can we get the contact information for this young woman?"

"See, there's the rub," Fred said. "Darcy and I were supposed to meet her here today. This is the only free clinic that we know of in the Buffalo Creek area. Darcy went ahead and took the appointment that we'd set up for Jennifer."

"Maybe Jennifer got cold feet," Colt said. "Maybe she decided to go take the doctor up on the offer."

Maren's stomach twisted. She hoped this Jennifer hadn't contacted Derek Rolls. "Fred, it's imperative that we get a hold of Jennifer. Would you be willing to call her?"

Fred scrambled to bring his phone from his pocket, and he dialed the number. "Darcy's been calling her all morning. She hasn't picked up. We left messages. But I can certainly try again."

Sending up a small plea to God, Maren held her breath as the phone rang on speaker.

Just as Maren's hopes were plummeting, a soft woman's voice answered, "Hello, Fred. I'm sorry I didn't make it to the clinic. I've just been too sick to leave the house."

Maren didn't know the intricacies of pregnancy, having never been pregnant before, but she'd heard how debilitating morning sickness could be. "Jennifer, my name is Officer Maren Anderson. I'm with the Colorado K-9 Unit. It's very important that we speak to you about the doctor who approached you."

"Oh, him," Jennifer said with surprise in her tone. "He gave me the creeps. I have his card here. Do you want me to give you the information off of it?"

Maren barely contained her excitement. "I would indeed. Please."

"The card says his name is Dr. D. Rolls. It gives an address." She gave the number for a location in Colorado Springs. "There's a phone number here, too."

Eli took down all the information in his notebook.

"Jennifer, you've been a big help," Maren told the young woman. "It sounds like Fred and his wife want to help you. I hope that you will let them. Don't call that number or go with any strangers at all."

"Okay. I won't." There was no mistaking the wary concern in Jennifer's tone.

"Maybe you and Fred can reschedule your visit here to the Buffalo Creek free clinic," Maren told her, then hung up. Looking to Fred, Maren said, "Thank you for your cooperation. We appreciate it."

With that, Maren turned with Haven at her heels and headed for the exit. An urgency to get to that address provided by Jennifer had shivers of dread racing along her limbs. What would they find when they arrived?

"This could be the break we need," Eli said as soon as they hit the pavement outside of the Buffalo Creek free clinic.

Trying not to let her hopes rise, Maren paused on the sidewalk. "We need to call Emmett with an update. I'm hoping we find my sister and Mia there." Maren sent up a quick prayer for Mia and her own missing sister. Her pregnant twin. Her heart contracted within her chest. She rubbed at the spot concealed by the flak vest she wore. Another thought emerged. "Or other missing young women we aren't aware of yet."

The urgency to find the two missing women, along with any additional ones, and their unborn babies, had Maren's blood racing. She sent another prayer to God asking for protection for the innocent lives that were being used for criminal purposes.

Eli made the call to their boss and within a half hour, the Colorado K-9 Unit task force was mobilizing to descend on the address in Colorado Springs. She and Colt would meet them there.

Her nerves stretched taut with each passing mile as she sat in the passenger seat while Colt drove them toward the address. Behind them, Eli followed in his vehicle.

"We need to get this guy. We need to find Mia," Maren stated as she played with the cross around her neck. She needed to find her sister. "You think there's any possibility that Opal could've found out about this supposed free clinic and gone there after Barren Valley? Like Jennifer, had Opal been approached by Dr. Rolls and had she thought him creepy? But maybe she decided to go to the clinic he'd told her about since she had to flee the Barren Valley Clinic when the gunfire started."

"Anything is possible," Colt replied.

She stared out the window, the landscape becoming a blur as she lifted a prayer of safety for her sister and for Mia. Thankfully, the miles passed by quickly. They were set to join up with the rest of their team at a neutral spot near their target, after they'd checked out their quarry.

Colt drove slowly past the supposed free clinic on the outskirts of Colorado Springs, whose address Jennifer had given them from Dr. Rolls's card. The clinic wasn't in a medical office building but rather in what looked like a small private house on a residential street. The place was worn, with chipped paint, warped stairs and a few windows boarded up. Warning bells clanged in Maren's head.

"No way is this the clinic." She couldn't imagine her sister ever agreeing to enter a place so obviously neglected.

"Desperate people aren't worried about aesthetics," Colt said as he sped up and drove to the supermarket a half mile away, where they were meeting the other members of the task force.

She blew out a breath at the truth in his words. The thought of her sister being desperate was a stab to the heart. And that Opal hadn't felt safe enough to reach out was an even deeper pain. They were sisters. Didn't Opal know Maren would always have her back?

Apparently not.

Shame and regret twisted her up inside like a pretzel.

He parked and they climbed out of the vehicle, leashed up their dogs and met the others.

The task force leader, Emmett, was already there with his K-9, a female, brown-and-white Newfoundland named Gemma, who specialized in snow and water rescue.

Emmett was setting up a command post at the back of his rig while Gemma supervised.

Maren watched as K-9 Officer Autumn Riley of the Canyon Creek PD approached. Tall and fit in cargo pants and a T-shirt with the task force logo on the pocket, the blonde cop strode over with her partner, a male bloodhound named Bear.

A shudder of dread prickled Maren's skin. She hoped Bear's specialty skill of cadaver detection wouldn't be necessary today.

Lizzie and her retriever, Reena, arrived along with K-9 Officer River Jameson of the Ridge PD. River, a tall, blue-eyed officer, and his female yellow Lab, Frankie, were rock stars at search and rescue.

Two more vehicles arrived. The first contained dark-haired and dark-eyed, Lavender PD K-9 Officer Trevor Slate, with his female English springer spaniel, Lark. They worked the arson cases. And from the last vehicle exited Boulder PD Detective and K-9 Officer Melody Rust, a redhead with bright hazel eyes, and her male chocolate Lab, Dusty. Dusty was trained in detecting explosive materials.

They all gathered around the task force leader. Anticipation hung heavy in the air. This could be the biggest break yet in finding Mia and solving the case.

"We'll split up into groups," Emmett said, and divided the members. "Trevor, you're with me. We'll approach from the east side of the house. Lizzie and Autumn, you circle around the block and come at the house from the west. River and Melody approach from the rear," Emmett instructed. "Maren and Colt, make your presence known at the front door."

Trevor stepped forward with several evidence bags. "We'll have each of our partners, of the four-legged type," he said with a grin at Maren and Colt, "sniff from each of these bags. We need to at least know if any of the deceased women were ever in the house. Or if Mia Andrews is still there."

Maren wished she had something of her sister's to offer for the K-9s to sniff. But she didn't. She would have to be content with visually searching for Opal.

After all the dogs were given an opportunity to sniff from each bag, Emmett handed out earpiece communication devices. "Wait for my signal. Once Maren and Colt have initiated contact, we move in. If anyone tries to leave, take them into custody."

"You got it, boss," several task force members said as they dispersed into their groups.

Maren and Colt decided not to drive up to the house but rather walk. They cut through the parking lot and down the alley behind the grocery store. In tandem, with their dogs at their heels, they made their way to the door.

Colt remained a step behind Maren. "You do the honors."

Taking a breath to calm her racing heart, she rapped her knuckles on the door and then stepped back, putting her hand on her sidearm. So much was riding on this moment. Mia, Opal or others could be held hostage on the other side of that door.

Fragile hope hovered but could shatter at any moment like spun sugar. The deep longing to see her sister, to make sure she was safe and unharmed, created more tension, tightening Maren's shoulders.

The need to find Mia was a palpable entity that made Maren antsy. Her fingers flexed on the butt of her weapon as the silence stretched.

After several long moments without any sign of life inside

the house, Colt stepped forward. Anticipating he was going to try the knob, Maren opened her mouth intending to caution him to check for booby traps, when he squatted down and used a penlight to check the door's threshold, shining the light up and around the doorframe.

Maren nodded her approval as he checked for wires to make sure the door wasn't going to explode in their faces if they opened it.

He stepped back. "It's not rigged as far as I can tell."

"Doesn't mean it still isn't," she said. She shuffled Haven off to the one side of the wall next to the door and Colt did the same.

"We're going to breach," Maren told the team through the communication piece lodged in her right ear.

Emmett's voice rang clearly in response. "Go for it."

Since Colt was on the side of the door's handle, Maren gave the nod, and he reached forward with a piece of cloth that would protect his fingers in case there was any sort of poisonous substance on the metal. He twisted the knob and pushed the door open while at the same time turning away and bracing.

Maren also turned away and counted to ten. When nothing happened, she peeked around the doorjamb into a very barren-looking house.

Disappointment and frustration ran rampant through her system. "Empty."

"Hold your position," Emmett said. "We're coming. Let Melody and Dusty clear the house before anyone enters."

Tugging their canines away from the open door, Colt and Maren waited on the sidewalk as the rest of the team descended. Melody and Dusty entered the house, looking for any evidence of explosives.

They returned a few moments later. "It's clean," Melody stated with a frown.

"Any signs of life?" Emmett asked as he charged up the porch steps toward the front door.

"Not that I can tell. Whoever was here was careful not to leave behind any visible trace," Melody said.

Exasperated at encountering another dead end, Maren entered the empty house and headed up the stairs with Haven. Colt and Rusk followed right behind her, while the others fanned out to let their dogs sniff every inch of the place.

Neither Haven nor Rusk alerted in the bedrooms on the second floor. All three were vacant. The house appeared abandoned.

In the farthest bathroom, Haven alerted at the side of the bathtub. Maren hurried to peer over the lip and discovered a discarded hand towel lying inside the bathtub.

With her heart rate speeding up, Maren told the group, "Got something."

Emmett and Colt hurried to her position with their canines. Both Rusk and Gemma let out a bark. The two dogs were also alerting on the towel.

Putting on rubber gloves she'd grabbed from her pocket, Maren lifted the discarded towel. "Haven alerted. I don't know whose DNA is on this, but it has to be someone's scent held within one of the evidence bags. Maybe this wasn't a clinic, per se, but more of a holding ground until they could move the women to a medical facility."

"Sound reasoning," Emmett said. He took the towel, put it into a new evidence bag with gloved hands and signed his initials to the outside. Maren did the same.

"I'll have this analyzed and find out whose DNA is on it," Emmett said. "Eva's already working on finding out who owns this house. Let's canvass the neighborhood and see if anybody has seen something or knows anything that's useful."

Glad to be out of the depressing structure, Maren, with Haven, Colt and Rusk, headed down the street.

Before they approached a neighboring house, a wave of despair and anxiety about her sister's well-being crashed over

Maren, pricking her eyes with the burn of tears. Fear for not only her sister, but her sister's child, dug into her mind.

Growing up, Maren had been the strong one of the two of them. The one Opal had always turned to for comfort. They were stronger together than apart. Until their parents' death.

Opal had turned inward, withdrawing from everyone, even Maren, while Maren's rage at the injustice of the person getting away with murder had spurred her to push forward, excelling at school and then the police academy.

She could see now how single-minded she'd been, using academics and the drive to become a police officer as her way of coping with their deaths. Opal had eventually started using drugs to numb her grief.

Neither of them had sought help or found comfort in each other. They'd drifted apart until Opal cut ties and disappeared. And now she was on the run with bad people after her.

"Opal must feel so alone..." Her voice broke. "Dead to everyone who knew her, with nowhere comforting to turn. Not even me."

Colt halted as Haven whined and brushed up against her legs. The dog seemed to always sense when Maren was upset.

"You can't give up hope," Colt said. "We'll find her."

He slid an arm around her shoulders and drew her close. The warmth of his bigger body wrapped around her, soothing her pain. For a moment, she rested her head on his shoulder, realizing how far she'd come to be able to trust this man. "Thank you. I needed to hear that."

He was silent for a moment, then patted her shoulder before releasing her and stepping away.

A coldness seeped in. Unaccountably, she missed the anchoring effect he provided. The steadiness of his close presence.

"Right now, we have to focus on the investigation at hand," he said, his tone all business now. "We know one of the baby smuggling victims was in that house because the dogs all alerted to a scent. Which victim remains to be determined but all the victims deserve our full attention."

He and Rusk strode off, leaving Maren to stare at his retreating back with a surprising amount of hurt crowding her chest. She couldn't help but feel that he was withdrawing emotionally from her, as if comforting her had been too much for him. Knowing how badly he'd been burned by his last romantic partner, she understood his caution. But they weren't romantically involved.

Unless he was afraid that she'd become too attached because of his efforts to offer solace?

No worries there.

She would emulate his guarded demeanor. Keeping a barrier up between them would be in both of their best interests. They were working a case and needed to keep their judgment clear. No emotional entanglements.

The last thing she needed right now was to fall for her temporary partner. Her heart had been closed off for so long after the deaths of her parents, her uncle and then believing Opal was gone, that she didn't know if anything could pry her heart open again.

ELEVEN

Two hours later, after a thorough canvassing of the neighborhood and the businesses within a one-mile radius of the house that was being used as an OB clinic, they had very little information to go on.

One neighbor reported there were all sorts of shenanigans going on in the middle of the night at the address Jennifer had relayed to them. But the neighbor didn't see so well in the dark and couldn't give any description of those going in or out of the house. No one else in the area seemed to know who owned or resided in the place.

Colt hated the sense of defeat invading his chest, the feeling of being no closer to discovering information on the whereabouts of Dr. Rolls, the baby smugglers or the missing woman, Mia Andrews.

The defeat mingled with his frustration and rage at not being able to find Shadow. Or Opal. The image of the despair in Maren's eyes filled his mind, twisting his heart. He'd taken her into his arms to offer his support and had found himself not wanting to let her go. He was growing attached and was at risk of becoming too close to her, too involved.

He had to keep her at a distance. But he found that keeping his guard up was becoming harder with every moment they spent together. After the betrayal of Rebecca, he'd promised himself he wouldn't give anyone the power to hurt him again. Even if Maren wouldn't purposely break his heart, getting heartbroken again was a fate he'd do anything to avoid.

His mood darkened as they headed back to the SUV.

The loud grumble of his stomach had her turning toward him with a raised eyebrow.

"There's a diner I know of where the owners let the K-9 handlers and their dogs eat inside," she told him. "It'll get us out of this heat. And it's safe. Lots of law enforcement eat there, so we'll have built-in backup."

That sounded good to Colt. He knew she'd be anxious to find her sister, but this morning's search had been exhaustive, and they did need to eat. Also, it would provide a distraction so he couldn't analyze the emotional turmoil going on inside him regarding Maren. That would be a good thing. Seeing her so distraught and down over the plight of her sister tore him up inside. Offering comfort to her seemed natural and right.

Just as almost kissing her the night before had.

But he needed to keep his perspective straight. He wasn't ready to allow his heart free rein. There was too much at stake. And he would return to Denver when this partnership was over, while she would stay with her task force and eventually return to the Colorado Springs Police Department.

There just didn't seem to be a future for them. The thought left him feeling empty in a way he hadn't in a long time, if ever. It made no sense. They'd only recently met. Sure, he liked her, trusted her and cared about her well-being. But that was what one did with a partner, right? Didn't mean there was anything romantic about his feelings.

Thankfully, by the time they made it to the diner the lunch crowd had dispersed and there was an empty booth in the back. He and Maren slid into a corner, their dogs at their feet, where they could watch the front entrance, the back entrance and the window that faced the street.

There would be no surprises for them while they ate lunch.

They both quickly ordered. Colt opted for a hamburger and fries while Maren chose a grilled chicken sandwich and coleslaw. The waitress brought over bowls of water for the dogs, which both canines lapped up eagerly.

"Can I give them each a pup cup?" the waitress, whose name tag read Heleene, asked.

"Rusk will love you for the rest of your life," Colt told her.

"Haven will be equally enamored," Maren said.

Heleene retreated, returning a few minutes later to give each dog a small paper container filled with whipped cream.

The dogs settled in to lap up their treats.

An awkward silence descended between Colt and Maren. He wasn't quite sure how to breach it. Staying focused on their cases seemed like the best idea. "Tell me about your team members," he asked.

She cocked her head with a smile. He realized he was taking a note from her playbook when she'd asked him to tell her about his family. He'd understood then that she hadn't wanted to be the one talking.

"I'll tell you everything I know," she said. "We've only been a team for three months now. I haven't delved too much into anyone's personal stories."

Remembering she had mentioned that they shared the grief bond, he said, "Tell me about Eli."

"I only know there's some tragedy there. No details."

While she talked about each of the team members, giving very brief information that she knew about where the person was from and the specialty of their K-9, Colt found himself mesmerized by her voice.

Affection swelled within his chest. She paid attention to the details. He liked that about her and he trusted her in a way he hadn't trusted anyone other than family.

But could he trust his heart? Could he open up and let her in?

The memory of his bad judgment where Rebecca was concerned rose in his mind like a large stop sign.

Their food came, and he dove in with gusto, thankful for the time to process and corral his emotions.

They both cleared their plates and shared a laugh.

"I won't need to eat until breakfast," Maren said.

"We'll see about that," Colt told her. "Room service might have something appetizing in several hours."

"Too true." She slid out of the booth.

As he moved to slide from the seat, his phone rang. Seeing his mother's number had him pausing. "My mom again."

Maren resumed her seat. "Take it."

"I know why she's calling." He sighed and pressed the answer button. "Mom."

"Just reminding you—"

"I know what day it is," he said. "My job has been very consuming. I don't know if I'll make it."

Across the table from him, Maren's eyebrows dipped with curiosity. Then she looked away to stare out the window.

On the other end of the line, his mother huffed out a breath filled with exasperation. "You need work-life balance."

"Mom, there is no such thing." At least not for him, there wasn't. He had no life outside of his job.

Well, except for his family, but he already gave them Sunday afternoons.

"Now, what kind of attitude is that? You'll never have your own family if you continue to think that way," his mother chided.

He hated disappointing her, but he doubted having a family of his own would ever happen. His parents were going to have to be content with his siblings and their families.

"You can take an hour break from your job to wish your nieces happy birthday," his mom continued. "I reminded you about their party."

He pinched the bridge of his nose. "What time again?"

"Six p.m. for dinner and cake immediately after, but you should come earlier to visit." There was a smile in her voice that had Colt shaking his head.

So much for the hour she mentioned.

He glanced at Maren, who now had her elbow on the table and her chin resting on her fist. She looked so dejected. His heart ached for her. "Do you mind if I bring a colleague?"

Her gaze snapped to him.

"If it gets you here, you can bring the whole DEA office for all I care," his mother said tartly.

He chuckled, knowing she meant it. "There will just be one other person."

"Don't forget to stop and get presents for your nieces," his mother instructed before hanging up.

Colt groaned. Another thing he'd forgotten. Presents. He loved his twin nieces. They were such rays of sunshine. He'd been so focused on bringing down Shadow and finding Opal and now with the task force and Maren… He was feeling stretched in all directions.

He tucked his phone away into a pocket.

Tension gripped him. He'd committed him and Maren to going to his nieces' birthday party. Would Maren be agreeable?

"I know this is a big ask, but would you be willing to accompany me to my twin nieces' birthday party for just a couple of hours? Long enough to have a slice of cake and say happy birthday."

Her blue eyes widened, and her mouth formed an O. "When?"

"Tonight. But first we have to stop by a store and get them presents."

"Wouldn't attending the party put your family in jeopardy?"

"I'd thought about that, but my parents have a security system and we'd have the dogs to alert to any danger."

She played with the cross at her neck. “Are you sure your family would be okay with me joining you?”

“Yes, of course,” he was quick to assure her. “As I’ve already told you, they love having guests.”

“Your parents maybe, but your nieces?” The skepticism in her voice rang clear. “Would they really want a stranger crashing their celebration?”

“Trust me, they will love you.” He searched her face, trying to determine what she was thinking that put a worried expression on her pretty face. Was it insecurity? Which didn’t seem right for the woman he was coming to know. Would seeing his twin nieces be painful for her? “If you’d rather not, I can beg off.”

“Oh no. You should definitely go. You could drop me off at the hotel,” she said.

The thought of letting her out of his sight, of her potentially being vulnerable, squeezed his chest tight. Giving a negative shake of his head, he said, “I’d prefer we didn’t split up.”

Her teeth tugged at her bottom lip. His gaze followed the slight movement. The yearning to lean forward and kiss away the worry furrowing her brow flooded his system.

He cleared his throat to tamp down the urge. “We have a couple of hours,” he said. “Take your time in deciding.”

She reached across the table to place her hand over his. “I’d like to go. Thank you for including me.”

Meeting her gaze, he delved deeply into the warmth he found there and wondered just how smart inviting her had been. But splitting up was not a viable option. If Shadow came after Maren again and he wasn’t there to help…if something happened to her, he would never forgive himself.

Several hours later, they returned to the hotel so they could freshen up and change clothes before heading to the birthday party. Maren nervously put on a summer dress that she had impulsively packed when she'd left her town house. She brushed her hair, allowing the long honey-colored waves to glide down her back. She applied lip gloss and felt ridiculous for the effort.

This wasn't a date. Even though they were headed to Colt's family event, they were colleagues sticking together for safety reasons. Nothing more.

Waiting to hear back from Vinnie Homer about her sister had Maren on edge. She'd checked in with the US Marshals to no avail. No contact had been made yet.

She lifted up a quick prayer that the hand towel Haven had found would yield some useful results, but those would take time. But she did call Eva to ask about Colt's phone being tracked. Eva had confirmed a spam call to his phone had planted malware that had allowed someone to track him, but she was having trouble finding the source. Also, the burner phone they'd confiscated off the assailant at the river hadn't yielded anything useful. The calls in and out were to more burner phones, all of which were currently turned off. But Eva had a special program to alert her if any were turned back on and promised to give Maren a call if it happened.

Without any leads to go on, though, or any idea where either of the young women were, Maren and the task force had no choice but to continue their search for another clue. They'd canvassed the area around the motel in Barren Valley, then headed back to Colorado Springs to connect with the last place Opal had worked, but the fast-food joint hadn't proved fruitful. By late afternoon, Maren's fatigue had her head pounding and her heart aching.

Going to Colt's family event was a welcome distraction, even if she was nervous about attending.

Having tucked some essentials in her backpack in case they were called to a case, she slung the bag over her shoulder and led Haven into the hallway to wait for Colt. When he stepped out of his hotel room, her heart skipped a beat. He'd changed into khaki shorts, casual tennis shoes and a button-up blue shirt with fish all over it. A price tag hung from the sleeve opening.

"Are you planning to return the shirt?" Suppressing a smile, she pointed to the tag.

He grinned. "Oops. I'll have to cut it off when we get to my parents'."

"I might have something that will work." She dug through the backpack pockets and produced nail clippers. "These will do." She snipped the plastic thread securing the tag to the shirt.

"I guess we're going incognito?" she asked as her gaze landed on Rusk, who no longer had his DEA vest on. It was stored in the SUV.

"If you'd prefer for Haven to wear hers, that's fine."

"I'm sure she'd be okay without it," Maren told him. "It makes her hot." She quickly took off Haven's police vest and stuffed it into the backpack.

Once they were in the SUV and rolling along, Maren couldn't stop fidgeting.

Colt reached across the seat to briefly touch her knee. "Hey, it'll be okay. No need to be nervous."

Easy for him to say. Though she didn't mind crowds or being part of a group of law enforcement, she wasn't used to big family gatherings. Even as a kid, it had always just been her parents and sister, with her uncle occasionally joining them for holidays.

On the way, they stopped at a store and bought two age-appropriate board games, one for each twin, and put the games into sparkly birthday gift bags with pink tissue paper. Colt bought two different cards and signed his name. He stuck one into each bag without putting which girl it was for.

"They'll share the games," he assured Maren. When she arched an eyebrow at him, he asked, "Is that a mistake?"

"No, actually, it's very thoughtful of you." And very sweet. Unexpected from such a no-nonsense, tough officer of the law. "When Opal and I were kids, we'd get one gift to share because my parents didn't want us fighting over them. But it only made receiving gifts sort of a letdown. Opal and I would take turns opening the one gift each year. It wasn't enjoyable."

"You deserve to be showered with gifts," he said, then looked startled as if he hadn't meant to say what he had out loud. "I mean, you and Opal should have been given lots of gifts. Every kid deserves to have presents on their birthday."

"Nice recovery," she teased, enjoying the way his cheeks above his beard pinkened.

And she couldn't deny she found the sentiment of his words rather nice. Not that he meant anything more than what he'd added about children deserving gifts. He'd just had a slip of the tongue. He couldn't have meant he wanted to give her gifts. That would be…thrilling. Exciting and sweet. And way out of bounds.

She needed to stay focused on what was important. Opal. Mia. Taking down Shadow. Finding Dr. Derek Rolls and ending the illegal baby smuggling ring.

She carried the presents to the SUV and hoped attending this party was the right thing to do, because she couldn't shake the gnawing worry camping out in her gut.

The Dawson clan lived on the outskirts of town on a sprawling ranch. A large, two-story main house built of stained natural wood with dormer windows and a peaked roof sat center stage at the end of a long driveway. Various types of trees provided shade for the house and a corral. Fenced pastureland with grazing horses stretched far and was dotted with several outbuildings.

Surprise arced through Maren. "Did you grow up here?"

"I did. You like?"

"Yes. It's beautiful." She stared at him. "Are you a cowboy?"

"Reformed."

His grin did funny things to her insides. She laughed to cover his effect on her. "Is there such a thing?"

"According to my father, yes." Colt slowed the vehicle and eased it to a halt next to several large trucks and SUVs of various sizes. "He'd prefer I wore my rodeo buckle and cowboy hat all the time. But I'd stand out. I'd rather blend in."

"Wait. Aren't rodeo buckles trophies? Meaning you've won a rodeo?" She knew nothing about the cowboy way or rodeos.

"I've had my share of good rides," he said with a shrug.

She liked his humility. "Doing what?"

"Riding broncs both saddle and bareback," he said. "Did I forget to mention that my family raises and trains rodeo bucking horses?"

Another laugh escaped her. "Yes, you did forget to mention that." Fascinated, she viewed him in a whole new light.

There were more facets to this man than she'd originally thought. And with each revelation of character, she was finding herself drawn more and more to him. Anticipation of learning additional tidbits about him had her actually excited for the evening as he helped her from the vehicle.

Instead of going through the front door as she expected, he led her around to the enormous back patio, which was filled with balloons in every shade of pink she could imagine. Children of all ages ran around the expansive lawn, taking turns chasing each other. A large, inflatable bounce house was off to the side. And a bubble machine sent translucent circles into the air.

Sitting at tables on the patio were at least two dozen adults. Maren's steps faltered. This wasn't just family, these were friends. Friends of the Dawsons and their children. Talk about being thrown into the deep end.

A squeal of delight went up as a woman in her mid-sixties came out of the house through the open French doors. She was beautiful with light auburn hair streaked with gray and cut at her chin. She had the same green eyes as her son. She wore wide-legged linen pants in a soft green, with a flowing, flowered top. "Colt, you made it."

"Hey, Mom." Colt hugged her.

Maren ached in a strange way to see the bond between Colt and his mother.

He released his mother, who immediately bent to lavish some love on Rusk. The dog's tail swished side to side.

"Mom, this is Officer Maren Anderson, and her K-9, Haven," Colt said. His mother straightened with a smile. "Maren, this is my mother, Dottie Dawson."

"Hello, Mrs. Dawson," Maren said.

"Hello, dear. Please, call me Dottie. We're so glad you could join us." She eyed Haven. "How old is Haven?"

"She's three," Maren glanced at her K-9, who sat staring at all the children running around.

"May I?" Dottie asked.

Maren nodded.

Dottie put out her hand for Haven to sniff before running her hand over Haven's sleek coat. "So soft." She met Maren's gaze. "Make yourself at home, dear. I need to check on my pies." Dottie strode away and disappeared back into the house.

Several people approached, hugging Colt and giving her a once-over.

Snagging his arm, a woman who looked like a younger version of Colt with long copper hair smiled. She had on a Broncos football T-shirt and shorts. She wasn't as tall as her brother but close. "Who's your *friend*?"

The way she emphasized the word *friend* made Maren blush. The implication was that she and Colt were something other than platonic. They all thought he'd brought a date. What was she going to do? How should she handle this?

She had no idea.

If only she and Colt had met at another time, under different circumstances, who knew what might have developed between them.

TWELVE

Before Maren could formulate words, Colt said, "This is Officer Maren Anderson of the Colorado Springs PD. Maren, my baby sister, Samantha."

Samantha grinned. "Mom said you were bringing a colleague. But wow, big brother." She bumped him with her hip, then stuck out her hand for Maren to grasp. "You can call me Sammy."

Shaking the woman's hand, Maren said, "Nice to meet you, Sammy."

Two little identical girls, with big hazel eyes, strawberry blond hair and matching pink dresses, ran up, each grabbing a hold of one of Colt's legs.

The twins looked up at him and said in unison, "Uncle Colt."

"Maren, this is Ivy." Colt put his free hand on the girl to his left's head. "This other rascal is Fiona."

Though the twins were identical, Ivy had a purple ribbon in her hair while Fiona had a yellow ribbon. Maren's mother used to do the same by putting different hair ties or barrettes in Maren's and Opal's hair so that people could identify them without always having to ask which was which.

Of course, Maren and Opal, usually at Opal's urging, would switch their identifying markers or ditch them altogether. Drove their mother to fits. Now, as an adult, Maren regretted the childhood pranks she and Opal would play on their parents, teachers and strangers alike.

The girls blinked up at her, curiosity evident on their sweet faces. It was on the tip of her tongue to tell the girls she was also a twin, but with her emotions so close to the edge, she wasn't sure she could without shedding a tear.

"I like your dresses," Maren told the girls.

"Thank you," the two said in unison.

Maren remembered a time when she and Opal had been perfectly in sync. A pang hit her chest. She missed her sister.

Another woman with dark mahogany hair held back by a clip and wearing a blue skirt, sandals and white tank top approached, snagging Colt's free hand. She gave Maren a curious glance and smiled. "I'm Abigail. The twins' mom."

"My other sister," Colt said. "Abby, this is Maren." Colt gave Maren a sheepish smile. "My brothers are around here somewhere. I'm sure you'll meet them soon."

Samantha looked to Haven. "Is your K-9 friendly?"

"She is when she's not working," Maren replied.

The twins turned their gaze on her. "Can we pet her?"

Since Haven had little experience with kids, Maren crouched down next to Haven and put a hand on her back, letting her know to stay calm. To the little girls, she said, "Let her sniff your palm before you touch her."

The twins held out their palms. Haven eyed them, then nudged each girl's palm with her nose before giving each a lick. The two little girls giggled. Then they turned their attention to Rusk and practically tackled the dog. The German shorthaired pointer pretty much flopped down and let the two girls crawl all over him.

Haven stood as if ready to defend her new friend.

"Playtime," Maren told Haven. The dog visibly relaxed and sat back on her haunches.

Laughing, Maren rose just as Dottie returned. "Colt, go check on your father." She gestured to the man at the grill and said to Maren, "That's Joe."

He was a barrel-chested man with a full head of white hair and an impressive mustache. He had on a plaid shirt underneath a black apron as he flipped burgers, hot dogs and steaks on the barbecue.

Dottie tucked her arm around Maren's. "Let me introduce you around."

For the next fifteen minutes, Maren was taken on a whirlwind tour through the party, being introduced to Colt's two brothers and their wives and the extended family, a couple of cousins, aunts and uncles, and friends.

Finally, Colt arrived at her side. "Mom, Maren and I would like a moment to decompress. Any chance you made strawberry lemonade?"

His mother scoffed. "Of course I made a strawberry lemonade." She winked at Maren. "My specialty."

Colt drew Maren off to the side to a quiet corner where they sank onto Adirondack chairs. Haven stayed at Maren's side, while Rusk ran around weaving in and out of all the children playing on the spacious lawn.

"Are all of your family gatherings like this?" she asked him. Her head was spinning with all the names.

"Only the special ones. And holidays, and most Sundays," he said with a grin. "My parents love to host. That's why they bought this spread when they married."

Taking in the grazing horses and the Rocky Mountains in the distance, she marveled at the stunning view and the peace of the land. "How many acres?"

"A hundred in total," he told her.

She didn't know much about ranching, having always lived

within the bubble of the city, but that seemed like a decent amount of land. "You learned to ride at a young age?"

"I did," he said. "Do you ride?"

"I rode a pony at a fair once," she admitted. "Not quite the same."

His chuckle sounded deep and pleased and reverberated through his chest. She liked the sound of it. She liked this relaxed version of him.

Yet, she couldn't settle the anxiety lurking at the edges of her mind. What was happening with her sister? Was she safe? What about Mia?

"Is it weird that I feel guilty enjoying myself?" she asked quietly. "Knowing my sister and Mia are out there, pregnant and scared?"

Colt reached across the chair to take her hand. "Not strange at all. But don't let the guilt or worry eat you. At the moment, the situation is out of our control. We have to trust God has them. We'll find them both. I promise."

She tilted her head. "You can't make that promise. No one can. Sometimes evil wins."

He sucked in a breath. "Unfortunately, that's true. But I refuse to give up hope." He rubbed his chin as if working something out in his head. His eyes took on a contemplative sheen. "Partnering with you the past couple of days has made me realize that even if bad things happen, or bad people happen, like Rebecca, not everything or everyone in life will be bad. Does that make sense?"

"It does," she said. "But I haven't figured out how to know the difference."

His expression cleared and he squeezed her hand. "I think that's where our faith comes in."

Her heart rate ticked up. There was so much about this man she admired, respected and liked. He was humble yet strong and determined. He was willing to adjust his course and his thought process as new information was introduced to him. Being here at his family's home made her want to belong.

Alarm bells clanged in her head. She was becoming emotionally entangled with her partner. A recipe that could end in disaster.

The twins ran over, stopping in front of Maren as she sat chatting with Dottie on the back patio of the Dawson ranch a little while later. "Uncle Colt said you're a twin."

Maren's gaze jumped to where Colt was talking with the twins' mother.

Focusing back on the two girls, she kept her emotions in check to admit, "I am a twin."

"Are you older?" Fiona asked. She pointed a thumb at her own chest. "I'm older."

"Just by two minutes," Ivy groused as only a newly six-year-old could.

Maren understood the struggle. Opal hadn't liked being the youngest either. "I'm older by three minutes."

Fiona stuck her tongue out at Ivy.

Ivy rolled her eyes at her sister.

Maren laughed out loud. The interplay was so familiar. She and Opal had once had that sort of relationship.

Ivy grinned, then asked Maren, "Where's your twin?"

Maren's heart gave a small bump as pain stabbed at her. If only she knew. Heart aching, she answered honestly, "At the moment, I don't know."

Both of their little faces scrunched up in confusion.

"Why not?" Ivy asked. "Don't you like her?" She slanted a glance at her sister.

"Of course she likes her," Fiona stated firmly. "They're twins. Like us. We like each other."

Ivy wrinkled her nose. "Most of the time."

Maren bit her lip to keep from laughing again. Oh, how she and Opal had quarreled as kids and teens. But at the end of the day, they were each other's best friend.

At least they were until they weren't. Until grief and choices separated them from each other, creating a chasm that Maren prayed could be repaired. How had she let life get to this point? She should have worked harder at being a better sister, better friend, to Opal. Then maybe she wouldn't be out there hiding, pregnant and alone. The burn of tears pricked her eyes. She blinked rapidly to keep them from showing.

"Girls," Dottie intoned a warning.

Hoping to thwart the argument she saw brewing between the girls and their grandmother, Maren said, "Being a twin is special. Sisters are friends forever. Don't ever let anything come between you."

If only she and Opal had adopted the philosophy of not letting anything come between them, then maybe Opal wouldn't have delved into drugs. Maybe she and Maren could have helped each other through the difficult days rather than turning away from each. If only…

There was no use looking at what-ifs. The past couldn't be changed.

The girls considered for a moment, then looked at each other as if in silent agreement. Maren had shared many a silent conversation with Opal as a kid. She'd thought that special bond was lost to her when she'd believed Opal was dead. But now there was a chance, no matter how slim, that she and Opal could get that back. That was if she and Colt could find her.

The twins walked away and were soon giving chase to a couple of boys.

Allowing her gaze to skate over the happy, smiling faces of both family and friends, she finally landed on Colt, and a deep sense of contentment tried to take hold. She fought against it. She couldn't let down her guard.

Colt met her gaze across the patio and the small smile he gave her brought heat to her cheeks, belying the conviction she needed to stay detached. She wasn't sure that would be possible as long as they worked together. Because he made her yearn for things, things like a home, children, family, in ways she never had before.

The burner phone in Colt's pocket buzzed. He retrieved the device and stared at a number he didn't recognize displayed on the small screen. Pushing the talk button, he said, "Agent Dawson."

"This is Agent Spares," a deep male voice said. "The boss wanted me to inform you that the blue panel van was found near Littleton."

Anticipation revved in his veins. It was the same van the shooters had been driving when they'd shot at Maren on the side of the road. "Did Forensics find anything useful?"

Maren, who'd joined him on the patio, stilled next to him, but she practically vibrated with interest.

"No, the suspects torched the vehicle," Spares said.

"Figures." Frustrated with the lack of progress, Colt thanked the agent and hung up. He relayed the info to Maren.

"Shadow's being careful," she said. "But eventually, he'll make a mistake. We need to find Opal. She can identify him and stop his reign of terror." Maren's agitation was palpable. "We should be out there searching for her."

Her obvious distress had him tied up in knots. "If we knew where to look, we would be searching for her. She could be halfway across the country by now. Until she makes contact with Vinnie, there's not much we can do."

She reached for his hand. "This waiting is so hard," she said, her voice breaking.

A rush of tenderness engulfed his system. "I know." He threaded his fingers through hers. He hated the circumstances but couldn't deny how right it felt to hold her hand. To soothe her.

Every moment he spent with Maren, his admiration and affection grew exponentially. His heart went out to her and he was loath to let her go.

THIRTEEN

The moon rose into the sky above the Dawson ranch, providing a soft glow to the night and silvering the pasture grass. The corral railing gleamed white, making the lone horse it contained appear otherworldly. Leaning against the top rail to watch the horse, Maren couldn't believe the day she'd had. Despite her worry over her sister and Mia, Maren had loved being here on the Dawsons' ranch, and they'd stayed longer than expected. Maren hadn't laughed so much in, well, she couldn't remember the last time. Over the last few months, ever since Opal's supposed drowning and since joining the task force around the same time, she'd been running on high alert and had not taken any time, until tonight, to ease the stress of loss and concern driving her.

Everyone at the ranch had been so friendly; the food was delicious, and the whole evening a wonderful distraction from the heartache of not knowing where Opal was, even though she and Colt both continually checked their burner phones for news from their bosses, the US Marshals and Eva. But thus far, their phones remained quiet after the one call about the van.

She glanced sideways at Colt, who stood next to her at the rail fence to the corral. Haven and Rusk lay quietly at their feet. They were the only remaining guests, as everyone else had left. The lone horse trotted in a circle, whining every time it passed

Colt. Or maybe the horse was protesting the presence of two unknown observers.

"Beautiful horse," Maren said. She hadn't understood why Colt had led her away from the house after everyone else had gone home, until he'd brought her to meet his favorite horse. A black stallion with a white star centered on its forehead.

"Meet Titan," he said.

"Are Haven and I upsetting him?"

"No, he's high-strung all the time," Colt replied. "He and I have won a lot of competitions together over the years."

She would have liked to see Colt competing. "Maybe he's happy to see you."

"I ride him every Sunday afternoon," he said. "I'm sure he's confused why I'm here on a Saturday."

She thought it sweet he'd believe the horse could tell the passage of time. "We'll have to come back tomorrow so you can exercise him. Maybe you could teach me," she said impulsively.

He laughed, a deep enjoyable sound. "I can teach you to ride, but not on Titan. We do have some geldings that are very docile that would be great for a beginner."

She wanted to bristle at the suggestion she couldn't handle the big black horse, but he was right, she couldn't. This horse was a champion. A newbie like her needed a plodding horse that wouldn't mind an inexperienced person on their back.

A yawn escaped her. "We have a long drive ahead of us," she said, though she was loath to leave the safety and peacefulness of the ranch. Guilt pricked her for the thought. Her sister wasn't safe. A shiver of dread mingling with the cool night air raced along her limbs.

"You're cold," Colt said. "I'll go grab a jacket."

Colt hustled toward the house before she could protest. Rusk stood but stayed in place.

Rubbing her arms, Maren gazed at the wonderful display of God's handiwork, admiring the twinkling stars. Being here was like stepping into some kind of alternative reality where nothing from the outside world existed. There was only this moment in time. The worry for her sister and for Mia hovered close, though, dimming her enjoyment. Staring up at the sky, she had to trust that God would keep both women in His care until they were found.

Movement in her peripheral vision snagged her attention. At the same time, Haven growled, clearly sensing the danger. Rusk also let out a warning howl, which turned into a low growl.

She glanced toward the shadowed side of the house. A dark figure moved along the edge of the wall toward the back.

A jolt of adrenaline had her heart pumping. Colt was in danger.

Knowing they'd both locked their sidearms inside the vehicle's built-in safe, she contemplated making a run for the SUV. But there was no time.

"Haven, Rusk, Attack."

The Doberman took off like a rocket. Rusk raced after her.

Maren followed at a run.

Floodlights came on, illuminating the outside of the house. An alarm blared.

The sound of a fight came from the backyard.

Concern and dread pushed at Maren as she rounded the corner.

Colt and the intruder were on the ground, wrestling for control of a gun.

The dogs barked, growled and snarled as they lunged at the assailant dressed from head to toe in black, with only his eyes revealed through the slits of a ski mask.

The alarm ceased and the back door opened. Joe, wearing lounge pants and a T-shirt over his barreled chest, rushed out with a rifle at his shoulder. "Colt!"

Maren jumped into the fray, helping Colt to secure the

weapon and subdue the intruder. They managed to force the man to his stomach.

Colt yanked the man's arms behind his back while Maren grabbed the Glock. "Joe, do you have any zip ties?"

"Would duct tape do?" the older man asked.

"Yes, Dad," Colt said.

Joe hurried inside as Dottie came out in a robe belted at the waist. "The security system alerted the police. They'll be here soon."

When Joe returned, Colt used the duct tape to secure the intruder's hands behind his back. Then he slipped the mask off the man's head.

Recognizing him as one of the men who'd attacked her at the river and then managed to make bail after being arrested, she couldn't keep the anger out of her voice as she asked, "How did Shadow know we were here?"

"I want a lawyer," the man said with a smug smile.

Gritting her teeth, she found it took all her restraint not to topple him over and tell Haven to attack again.

Shortly the police arrived and did a perimeter sweep to make sure the man had been alone. Not finding any more bad guys, the police took statements and hauled the assailant off to jail.

No doubt to be released on bail again. The burn of frustration had Maren rubbing her temples as she entered the house.

They gathered in the kitchen, and Dottie handed out mugs of hot chocolate. They all needed a moment to let the adrenaline from the intruder's presence ebb.

"How did Shadow's man know we were here?" Maren asked Colt. She sat at the counter and wrapped her hands around the mug, needing the warmth to chase away the cold seeping into her bones despite the moderate temperature of the house.

"We could have been tailed from the hotel," Colt replied. "Though I kept an eye out."

The self-recrimination in his tone had her touching his arm.

"This isn't your fault. Did you tell anyone you were coming? Or maybe one of the people at the party unknowingly let slip to someone in Shadow's organization that we were here."

"Only Emmett and my boss knew we were coming," Colt said. "I'd hate to think anyone we know might have ties to Shadow."

With a sigh, Maren turned to Dottie. "I'm sorry. We had no idea this maniac would attack here."

"Don't blame yourself, dear." Dottie put down her mug and gave Maren a hug. "Bad people will always find a way."

Unfortunately, there was truth in her words. Maren set aside her full mug. She couldn't take anything in at the moment.

"Well, now we know to be more cautious," Joe said. "I've reset the security system. Monday I'll have the security company put in sensors farther out on the property."

"I'm exhausted," Dottie said. "I'll take care of the dirty mugs in the morning."

"We should stay the night," Colt said. "Just in case more of Shadow's associates show up. I can't leave you unprotected."

"I agree," Maren said. They were both exhausted and worried. Staying the night seemed like the right thing to do.

After doing another perimeter check with the dogs, Colt and Rusk walked Maren and Haven to their room on the second floor. The soft cream carpet masked their steps. Wall scones threw an amber glow on the cream-colored walls.

"You okay?" he asked as they halted outside of the room.

Her natural tendency to balk at any hint she wasn't okay rose, but she tamped it down. His concern was genuine and warranted. "I will be once we find my sister and bring down Shadow. I hate that we brought trouble to your parents' house."

"I hear you," he said. "And we will succeed."

Taking solace in his confidence, she put a hand over his heart. "Thank you for bringing me here. For sharing your family. And for having my back."

He covered her hand with his and brought her knuckles to his lips. He placed a soft kiss against her skin and a shiver of delight spread through her. "My pleasure."

She felt a nudge at the back of her knee. Startled, she glanced down to see Haven had wedged herself between Maren and door. Was the dog pushing Maren toward Colt?

The thought was ridiculous. Yet, Maren swayed toward him. Suddenly wanting, no needing, to take a leap with Colt. Before she could talk herself out of giving in to the yearning rising through her, she slid her arms around his neck and drew him closer.

His arms came around her and pulled her flush against him.

Their lips met in a tender caress. He tasted of chocolate and yearning. He deepened the kiss, and she groaned as longing ignited deep in her heart. Affection flooded her veins. She couldn't remember the last time anyone had kissed her so thoroughly. She matched his intensity as her pulse raced and emotions swirled. His hands smoothed down her back. She tangled her fingers in his thick hair.

The kiss slowly eased and they drew apart. She couldn't catch her breath. Her heart felt too big for her chest.

He dropped his forehead to hers. "Good night."

With that, he released her and strode down the hall and took the stairs, disappearing from sight.

She touched her lips, felt the warmth of Colt lingering on her skin, and a gentle fondness spread through her.

What had she done?

Kissed him.

And she wanted to again.

Taking a shuddering breath, finally filling her lungs with air, she stared down at Haven. "I blame you."

Haven stared back, her brown eyes warm and completely unrepentant.

Maren dropped her head to the door. She was losing it if she thought Haven had somehow orchestrated that kiss. No, Maren had wanted to kiss Colt, and she had. Now she just needed to figure out how to deal with the burgeoning emotions crowding her heart.

FOURTEEN

The next morning, Maren attended an early church service with Colt and his parents, wearing the same sundress she'd worn the previous day. As she climbed back into the truck after the service, she told Dottie, "Thank you for inviting me today."

Colt sat beside her while his father and mother sat in the front seats.

Dottie twisted in her seat with a beaming smile. "I'm so glad you both decided to stay the night and come with us this morning. After the nastiness of the intruder, we all needed some inspiration today." Her gaze bounced between Maren and Colt before she turned around in her seat.

Maren didn't respond but glanced at Colt.

So far, she'd managed to avoid talking about the ramifications of the kiss. But eventually, they would need to address it. Only they had bigger concerns at the moment. Namely last night's intruder.

She had called Emmett first thing this morning before leaving the house and let him know the ranch had been compromised. She wasn't sure being so far from the task force was in the best interest of either investigation, and she needed to get back to Denver. Still, she was glad they'd set Joe and Dottie at ease by staying with them—last night had shaken them all up.

As much as she cared for the older couple, her mind was doing mental gymnastics trying to figure out the perfect way to make sure everyone got what they needed. The task force, the Dawson family, her sister, and Mia. Not to mention Colt. Suddenly overwhelmed, she sank deeper into the truck's leather seat.

If only the decisions could be easy… But she'd learned the hard way that life was rarely easy or fair. She sent up a silent plea to God for His strength and guidance.

Colt's phone rang. He glanced at the number. "Agent Spares."

Maren hoped the forensic team had found something in the burned-out van after all.

When they reached the Dawson home, Joe and Dottie climbed out, but Maren and Colt remained in the truck as Colt answered. "Agent Spares, what can I do for you?"

"Hey, so your informant," he said, his voice low and raspy, "he says he remembered something that he'll only tell the lady cop. I assume you know who he's referring to."

Surprise washed through Maren. She met Colt's gaze and saw the same curiosity in his green eyes.

"Yes, I do," he said cautiously. "But why can't he just tell you?"

"I don't know. He's your CI," Spares snapped. "Can you bring the cop here?"

"To the safe house?"

Excitement and anticipation flaring through her, Maren nodded vigorously to encourage Colt to say yes.

"I'll see if I can find her. You'll need to text me the address. And then we'll have to arrange for a new location for Steve."

"Yeah, we can do that," Spares said. "I'll send the info. Just park at the curb and come to the front door." Spares hung up.

"What do you think Steve remembered? And why will he only tell me?" Maren's breath hitched. "It has to be something about Opal. Maybe he thought of where she might hide."

She opened her door. Thankfully, she'd brought a change of clothes consisting of a COK9 Unit shirt, dark pants and tennis shoes in case they were called to one of the cases they were working. She didn't think arriving in a dress would be appropriate. Unfortunately, she hadn't brought a Kevlar vest with her. She prayed it wouldn't be needed. "I'll grab Haven, change clothes, and meet you at the SUV after you change and get Rusk."

Colt pulled to the curb outside of the nondescript house located in Boulder, Colorado.

There were no signs of life outside the house or through the curtained windows. But Colt checked the address again, verifying this was the safe house address that Agent Henry Spares had given him.

Uneasiness had been dogging him every mile he and Maren had traveled closer to where Steve Loren was being held in protective custody.

He glanced at Maren in the passenger seat. Her honey brown hair was pulled back. Like yesterday, she'd applied a little gloss on her lips before church. But she didn't need any enhancements. She was beautiful inside and out.

The more he came to know her, the more he respected and admired her. And he worried for her safety. He couldn't bear the thought of her coming to harm. Was he falling for her? That kiss last night had rocked his world.

There was no denying he found her physically attractive. He also found her to be a woman of substance, integrity and compassion. A woman worth taking a risk on.

But how did he trust his judgment? When he'd started a relationship with Rebecca, he would've never guessed she was hiding such a devious side. He didn't believe that Maren had a deceptive side. But only God knew what lurked in the hearts of people.

He felt Maren's stare and glanced at her. Sure enough, she

was looking at him as if she knew he was thinking about her. “I don’t like this. Why would Steve need to speak with you?”

“The guy’s a drug addict. Why does he do anything?” She popped open her door and stepped out. She’d changed into a pair of black, lightweight cargo pants and a COK9 Unit T-shirt. She looked lethal, all business and yet undeniably appealing. Like she had last night. He wasn’t sure if he’d initiated that kiss or she had, but when she’d slid her arms around him, he’d thrown caution to the wind and fully embraced the moment. Every barricade he’d ever erected around himself had crashed to the ground, leaving his heart exposed. Yet, he didn’t feel vulnerable. Instead, he felt invigorated. As if he’d had a reawakening. For too long, his heart had been dark. Rebecca’s betrayal had left him cold and afraid. But now…

He wasn’t sure what to think. Or feel.

There were too many variables and too much at stake for him to delve into the emotions stirred by Maren.

He hoped she didn’t have any regrets. The best thing would be to stay professional and get the job done. He reached for the door handle and got out.

“If whatever he has to say will lead me to my sister and you to Shadow, then we have to go,” she said, rounding the vehicle.

They had been rehashing the same argument for the last two hours. Trying to view this from every angle. Why hadn’t Steve just told Agent Spares what he wanted Maren to know? Why bring her all the way here? Was Steve working for Shadow? Was this a trap?

A steely resolve settled in his gut. “Be ready for anything.”

“Always.” She unclipped the safety strap on her holster at her hip. “Let’s get the dogs.”

Once they had the two K-9s leashed and in their vests, announcing they were working dogs, they headed to the front door.

“Why didn’t he have us come from the back? He said we should park at the curb and come to the front door.”

"I don't know. Maybe because you said Steve would need to be moved," Maren said.

On the threshold and about to knock, he felt a trickle of unease travel through him and he dropped his hand. He grabbed Maren's arm and pulled her away from the door. She tugged Haven to her side.

"We should call the task force," he said. "I don't like this. Emmett said whatever backup we needed, he would provide."

"But that will take time." Determination marched across her features. "We've stalled long enough. We need to know what your CI has to say."

She walked up to the door and gave a loud rap of her knuckles. Haven sniffed the door and sat, her ears pricked forward. Rusk stayed beside Colt but tension quivered in his body.

Seconds later the door swung open and Agent Daniel Russell stood there. He was without his jacket, revealing his shoulder holster and his hand on the grip. His white button-down shirt was open at the collar, revealing a gold chain and a smattering of dark hair curling over his body armor. The sleeves of his shirt were rolled up.

This was the first time Colt had seen the agent ever appear a bit disheveled. He was usually completely buttoned up and by the book. But Colt supposed being in a safe house with a druggie for any extended time could test anyone's patience.

"Come in. Quick," Daniel said. He quickly closed the door behind them. "We don't need to advertise our presence to the whole neighborhood. What are you doing here?"

The unease he'd felt on the way here turned to dread. "Where's Agent Spares? He called and said Steve had something to tell us."

Daniel frowned. "What? Why would he call you?"

"Where's Steve?" Maren asked as she walked farther into the living room.

"He's in the last bedroom with Agent Spares." Daniel gestured down the hall to several closed bedroom doors. "I'll bring them out."

Daniel stomped down the hallway, leaving Maren and Colt standing alone. A bad feeling invaded Colt's chest. Why were the two agents not in sync?

Colt remained in the entryway while Maren stood in the middle of the living room, facing away from the front window. The light-colored curtains were closed but still allowed a good deal of light to enter the house.

A red dot appeared on Maren's back. Just as Haven and Rusk both let out loud, vicious barks.

Lunging for Maren, Colt wrapped his arms around her and took her to the floor seconds before the bullet from a sniper rifle broke through the front glass window and embedded itself in the hardwood next to them.

"Kitchen," he yelled to Maren, allowing her to scramble away from him.

Grabbing both dogs by the collar and pulling them behind the kitchen counter, they hunkered down while more bullets pelted the house.

As they drew their weapons, Colt said, "We need backup."

Maren had her phone out and was already dialing the Boulder PD. "Officer in trouble. Shots fired. Need backup." She rattled off the address.

Gunfire from the back of the house echoed as several more rounds of bullets came through the window, pinning them down.

A man staggered out of the hallway, clutching his shoulder where blood seeped through his fingers.

Colt recognized Agent Henry Spares. The man tilted and fell to the ground.

Colt's stomach dropped. Where were Daniel and Steve?

Moving quickly, he grabbed Spares by the ankles and dragged him to safety behind the counter. Within moments, the sound of sirens split the air. A welcome relief to the barrage of gunfire happening both at the back of the house and in the living room.

Within moments, the gunfire went silent.

Daniel stormed down the hall.

"You were followed!" His bellowed accusation bounced off the walls.

"Could be somebody was watching the house," Colt countered. "We should have parked down the street and come through the back."

"Then why didn't you?" Daniel demanded.

Colt looked at the unconscious Agent Spares. "He told me to come through the front."

Daniel made a face. "No, he didn't. You must have mistaken what he said, because telling you to come in the front would be irresponsible and ridiculous. He better not die because of you." He pointed a finger at Colt.

Maren stood, keeping a wary eye on the window. "Where's Steve?"

"He took a bullet to the head." Daniel grabbed his phone. "I'm calling this in. There will be a price to pay."

Disbelief coursed through Colt. He needed to see for himself that Steve was dead. He hurried down the hall with Maren and the dogs on his heels. He heard Daniel's voice loud and clear inside the room.

"This is Agent Daniel Russell." He gave the safe house's address. "I need an ambulance here pronto. And put me in touch with Special Agent in Charge Leo Herman."

In the back bedroom, Steve Loren lay on the floor, a single gunshot to the head. The window was shattered, indicating the shots had come from outside. But something about this whole situation didn't sit well.

What had Steve wanted to tell Maren? Or was this all a ploy to get her here so Shadow could kill her and Steve? Was Agent Henry Spares involved in the deception?

FIFTEEN

The drive to headquarters was delayed because of traffic. A full team meeting had been called, and Emmett had lab results from their search of the house Derek Rolls had been linked to. Maren kept an eye out for any signs of trouble as Colt maneuvered the SUV through the line of vehicles clogging the road. She stared at the drivers of the other vehicles, not seeing anyone paying them any attention.

Undoubtedly, the other drivers were only worried about the report they had to write for their jobs, the columns that needed balancing or the children that needed tending to, while she was consumed with worry for her sister, for Mia, for Colt and for herself… Steve Loren had been killed and a DEA agent shot. She wasn't sure what she and Colt had walked into or who had set them up. There were so many unknown variables that made knowing whom to trust difficult.

When they arrived at the task force headquarters, Colt parked, and they released Haven and Rusk from the back of the SUV, then hurried into the training center to drop off the dogs. The tightness in her chest made her breathing shallow.

"Take it easy." Colt placed a hand on the small of her back as they headed upstairs to the conference room.

The concern in his voice clearly indicated she wasn't very good at hiding her nerves. For some unfathomable reason, she took comfort in his touch. He steadied her. Grounded her. Kept the anxiousness from becoming too overwhelming.

All the task force members were gathered around the conference room table, including their tech, Eva Gomez. Maren was surprised to see the wealthy benefactor of the task force, Dodger Andrews, present and seated at the head of the table. As always, he wore a fleece vest despite the heat outside and plain-front khaki slacks. His thick gray hair looked as if he'd run his hand through it in agitation.

Did his apparent unease mean that it was Mia's DNA on the hand towel Haven had alerted on?

A pang of sorrow zipped through Maren and burned the back of her throat. Mia had been a young innocent woman with her life ahead of her and her unborn child.

She and Colt took empty seats near the door. Maren leaned over toward Colt to say, "The older gentleman sitting at the head of the table is Dodger Andrews. He funded the task force. Mia is his granddaughter."

Colt whispered back, "I can only imagine how heartbreaking this is for him."

Maren didn't need to imagine, she was living it with every moment that her sister remained missing. Opal was out there somewhere, trying to evade Shadow and his network of minions. Understanding the kind of fear Opal had to be experiencing had Maren wishing with all her might she could wrap her arms around her sister to comfort her, to protect her and bring her home.

"Any word yet from Vinnie?" Maren whispered the question to Colt, though she knew he'd tell her the minute he heard anything.

He shook his head. His green-gold eyes held sympathy in their depths.

Emmett strode to the front of the room, drawing her attention away from Colt.

"I have news regarding the evidence collected by Maren and her partner, Haven," Emmett told the group.

All eyes turned to Maren. She smiled slightly and gave a nod to her boss. She hoped she appeared calm and collected, because inside, her stomach was cramping with anticipation.

"The hand towel found in the bathtub had DNA that matched that of Nina Olson."

Maren sucked in a sharp breath. Nina's body had been recovered five months before the task force was formed. The seventeen-year-old from Colorado Springs had been missing for ten months but hadn't been reported missing by anyone. As far as the authorities could tell, Nina had willingly left her home so no one in her life had suspected foul play. Until her body was discovered. The pathology on her remains showed she'd recently given birth prior to her death. But so far, law enforcement hadn't been able to identify her baby's father or the location of her baby. They theorized the infant had been adopted through illegal channels they still hadn't uncovered.

The news that the DNA matched Nina was a blow but also a blessing to Maren.

She hated to think of the young woman suffering, but not finding any of Mia's DNA still gave them hope that the young woman, due to give birth in four months, was alive. And possibly had never been at the dilapidated house they'd searched earlier.

Dodger Andrews rose to address the group. "I want to thank you all for your hard work. I know you've been looking nonstop for Mia. Her family appreciates it." A spasm of pain crossed his features. "It's hard to not lose hope."

A murmur went through the room as people voiced their heartfelt sentiments.

"We can't lose hope," Lizzie said.

"She isn't close to her due date," Autumn pointed out. "They won't do anything to her—" She broke off with a grimace.

Maren didn't need to hear the rest of her colleague's words to know Autumn was going to say those who were holding Mia wouldn't harm her until after the baby was born. That seemed to be these awful people's pattern.

Emmett held up a hand. "If you all will join me in a prayer for protection for Mia and any other young women who are being held hostage by this baby smuggling ring."

Agreement swept across the room.

Maren bowed her head and closed her eyes. Colt's fingers curled around her own. She squeezed tight as Emmett lifted up a prayer.

"Dear Lord, we come before You collectively asking for Your sovereignty and Your protection over Mia Andrews and any other young women who have been preyed upon by this evil that has invaded our state. Please show us the way. Guide our steps and lead us to victory. In Your Son Jesus's name, amen."

Maren murmured an amen and heard Colt do the same along with others around the room.

"Maren," Emmett said, drawing her attention. "Tell us how your investigation into your sister's disappearance is going."

Maren's stomach knotted. Colt gave her hand a squeeze before releasing his hold on her. She flexed her fingers, wishing she could hang on to him.

Slowly, she rose. "So far we know that the person responsible for my sister needing to disappear goes by the moniker of Shadow. We have no ID on this individual. He runs a large drug organization within our state." She gestured to Colt. "Agent Dawson here is with the DEA," she said for Dodger's sake. "He has been working diligently to bring down this drug trafficker. However, Shadow has been elusive and seems to always be one step ahead of law enforcement's efforts." Outrage and speculation raced through the room.

Maren waited a beat for the others to quiet down before she continued, "Somehow, my twin sister became involved with one of Shadow's top trusted men. But when she and her romantic partner wanted out of the drug trade, he was killed. My sister went on the run."

Taking a breath, she fought to keep her pulse from racing. "I've been mistaken, several times, for Opal. For obvious reasons," she said with a wry grimace. "But after the arrest of these last two assailants, I feel it's possible Shadow is now aware I'm not Opal, and will stop fixating on me and turn his focus toward finding Opal. We're doing everything we can to find her first."

"I heard you have a CI in custody." This from Trevor who addressed Colt.

Colt rose from his seat. "We did. Unfortunately, the safe house where he was stashed was hit and he was killed. A DEA agent was wounded. My CI is the one who led me to Barren Valley Clinic where I ran into Maren. But Opal slipped away."

"We also have another source close to my sister who has reached out to her. We are waiting for Opal to respond," Maren told the group.

"Aren't you afraid Shadow's men will get to this source?" asked Melody.

"We are," Maren replied, her gut churching with anxiety. "The US Marshals have him in custody. As far as we know, they have not been compromised. But according to Agent Dawson's now deceased CI, Shadow has informants in all areas of law enforcement. So, we can't be sure." Her gaze roamed over the room as an insidious suspicion reared up. Could one of these people be a mole for Shadow?

No. She couldn't think that. Emmett had vetted each and every one of the task force members. She trusted Emmett, relied on his judgment. She trusted her colleagues. She wouldn't let doubt and misgivings have any place in her mind.

"Does your missing sister have anything to do with the task force's investigation into the illegal baby smuggling ring?" Dodger asked.

Maren replied, “It’s possible that Opal was targeted and groomed by Dr. Rolls just like another pregnant woman, Jennifer, was. Our only link is that Opal was at a clinic where Rolls once worked, but perhaps he also gave her a business card for another free clinic that she may decide to surreptitiously visit the longer she’s in hiding.”

“If nothing else, we do know Shadow is very plugged in to the criminal underworld within Colorado,” Colt added. “He may know something useful. Which is another reason we are trying to find and arrest him.”

“The task force will be concentrating on finding Mia and breaking up this baby smuggling ring.” Emmett held Maren’s gaze. “Stay on finding your sister and arresting Shadow. If you need anything from the task force, please let us know.”

“I appreciate that, Emmett.” Maren couldn’t begin to express her gratitude.

Her loyalty was to the task force, but her sister was family. Finding her sister was her priority. And if there was a possibility that bringing down Shadow would help the task force in their mission, then she had to seize the opportunity. “You have no idea how grateful I am.”

“Okay, people,” Emmett said, addressing the room at large. “Let’s get out there and make headway on finding our missing mother-to-be.”

Slowly everyone filed out of the conference room. Maren and Colt along with several other task force members headed downstairs to the training facility to retrieve their K-9 partners.

Eli Blackwood stepped up and kept pace with Colt and Maren. “If there’s anything I can do, don’t hesitate to ask.”

Maren appreciated her teammate’s offer. She knew the Oak City officer who specialized in dangerous cases had dealt with some serious losses in his life. “Thanks, Eli.”

The trio stopped at the edge of the training ring to check on the progress of the two German shepherd puppies, Chance and Trooper. The balls of fluff were running around the ring, chasing each other with the high school volunteer, Jessie, running after them.

Dev, the lead trainer, came over to stand with them and watched the chaos of the two little German shepherds. "Chance is doing well. Progressing like his esteemed parents." He made a face. "Trooper's still a bit behind."

They watched as the puppies tumbled over each other. Dev let out a long whistle. Chance skidded to a halt and turned toward the sound. Trooper, however, continued to run, evading Jessie and racing toward the gate at the end of the ring.

Dev put out his hand and yelled, "Touch."

Chance raced across the training center to Dev's hand, popping his nose against Dev's palm.

Maren smiled. She loved to watch the trainers and the puppies. Her gaze tracked Trooper. "Uh-oh."

Trooper slipped between the small gaps of the gate and disappeared out of sight.

"Not a good sign," Dev said. "You three want to help find the little guy?"

"Do you mind if I release Haven?" Maren said. "It would be good for her to have some experience tracking the puppy."

"If you think she can be gentle when she finds him," Dev said. He looked to Colt and Eli. "Do your dogs need some practice?"

Eli chuckled. "Wrangler is always up for some fun."

Colt shrugged. "Rusk will do what he does. He's trained to track narcotics, not runaway puppies. But we'll give it a shot."

The three released their dogs from the kennels and put them on leads.

"Can he get outside?" Colt asked.

"At that end of the ring." Eli gestured to where Trooper disappeared. "The exit leads to the outdoor training yard."

He and his Belgian Malinois, Wrangler, walked through the

training ring and out through the gate where Trooper had escaped. Maren and Colt, with Haven and Rusk, walked around the outside of the ring, looking in the various open doors of the offices, the locker room and restrooms.

"Over here," Eli called. He and Wrangler found the puppy who had tunneled beneath a blanket in the far corner. Wrangler sat quietly as Eli pulled the blanket off the sleeping puppy.

Maren's heart melted. The snoozing puppy was adorable. Haven nudged the dog with her nose.

Rusk stood watching, his head tilting in curiosity.

Trooper woke up and let out a series of excited barks. He jumped to his feet and did figure eights between the bigger dogs' legs. Wrangler turned in a circle, keeping an eye on the pup. Haven danced aside then folded her legs into the down position, nearly sitting on Trooper.

Everyone laughed except for Dev, who gave a sigh. "This one might be pet material instead of a K-9 dog."

Handing Haven's lead to Colt, Maren scooped up Trooper and cuddled him close. "You are a sweet, sweet boy," she told the pup. "You're who you are and that's just fine."

She handed the young dog back to Jessie, who returned him to his crate.

Suddenly all the dogs turned and gave a bark of warning as three people walked into the center and stopped at the edge. Maren didn't recognize either of the two men or the woman who stopped a few feet away.

"The candidates for my job," Dev said. "Dodger Andrews asked me to watch each of the potential replacements work with Trooper and to report back with my assessment of them. They have their work cut out for them. Come, I'll introduce you." He walked toward the three people.

Maren didn't like the idea of Dev leaving. Since the day she'd arrived to be a part of the task force, Dev had been a wise and steady presence, making her and Haven feel welcome.

"Dev seems young to retire," Colt murmured.

"He wants to spend more time with his grandkids," she told him. "It's our loss for sure. But I trust Dev to find someone good."

"His decision, then?"

"From what I understand he'll have the final say," she explained. "But Emmett and Dodger will weigh in. Dev wouldn't leave us in a lurch. He'll pick the most qualified. And hopefully, one who will fit well with the task force members."

She assessed the three contenders. They all appeared to be in their early thirties. "Let's go meet them."

Leading their dogs over, Maren, Colt and Eli joined Dev and the others.

Dev introduced Maren, who in turn introduced Colt.

"This is Tanya Fielding," Dev said, gesturing to the petite redhead wearing cargo pants and a lightweight, long-sleeve shirt. "I've been working with Tanya at another facility for a year now."

Tanya's brown eyes were warm. "It's a pleasure. I'm in awe of the work the task force is doing."

"I'm Jacob Wexley. I'm a friend of Dodger Andrews." The man stepped forward, drawing their attention.

The pompous tone to his voice grated on Maren's nerves.

He continued, "I've been working with K-9 dogs across the state for the past few years."

"And this is Christian Dane," Dev referred to the last candidate who stood silently watching them all.

Maren exchanged a curious glance with Eli.

Colt's eyebrows rose. "Any relation to Emmett?"

The tall, muscular man gave a sharp nod. "Cousins."

Surprise had Maren considering the dark-haired, blue-eyed man more closely. She could see a resemblance now that she was looking for it.

"Okay, let's get to it, shall we," Dev said and urged his three potential replacements into the ring to work with Trooper.

"Seems all three of them have someone who's already involved in the task force rooting for them," Maren mused aloud to Eli and Colt.

"It will be a tough decision for sure," Eli said. "But it won't be made until November. They have time to prove themselves."

Leaving the training center, Colt and Maren headed back to the borrowed SUV.

"Colt." Maren paused at the back of the SUV. "Can you find out where Agent Spares was taken? Maybe he's regained consciousness and can shed some light on what Steve wanted to tell me."

Nodding, Colt released the hatch for Haven and Rusk to jump into the specialized compartment. "Good idea. I'll make the call."

SIXTEEN

"Thank you, sir." Colt hung up the phone after talking with his Special Agent in Charge Leo Herman. He turned to Maren, who stood outside the SUV, waiting for information on where the injured agent had been taken. Behind her, the task force headquarters' brick building gleamed in the afternoon sunlight. "Henry is at Boulder Memorial Hospital."

"Then off to Boulder we go." Her tone brimmed with anticipation.

He hoped she wasn't setting herself up for more disappointment. Henry had claimed when he'd called asking for them to come to the safe house that Steve refused to tell him why he had to talk to Maren. But if for no other reason than peace of mind, they needed to talk to the agent to verify if he knew something about the information Steve had, and why Henry had told them to come in the front entrance.

"My SAC also said they found a shooter's nest across the street from the house and one in the backyard," Colt said. "Forensics has collected bullets and are hoping to match them to other crimes."

"That would be a big break," she said.

Having already put the dogs in the specialized back compartment, Colt and Maren climbed into the SUV and drove away from the Colorado K-9 Unit task force headquarters. As they left Denver behind and the silence became too oppressive, Colt asked the burning question that had been plaguing him since the night before. “Are we going to talk about it?”

“Talk about what?”

The wariness in her tone let him know she knew exactly what he was talking about.

“The kiss.”

“We kissed,” she said, in a strained voice. “It doesn’t have to mean anything.”

He frowned as he changed lanes to pass a semitruck. He glanced in the rearview mirror, watching as various other cars made the same move. Was one following them? All things considered, his paranoia was justified. “Are you saying that because you think that’s what I want to hear? Or is that how you feel?”

“Does it matter?” From his peripheral vision, he noticed her shrug. But her hands twisted nervously in her lap.

His jaw tightened. After almost losing her, his feelings for her had clarified and expanded. But he needed to know how she felt. “It matters.”

She turned to face him in the passenger seat. He glanced at her, saw the worry in her blue eyes.

He faced forward and re-gripped the steering wheel. “I don’t regret it.”

“But you should,” she said softly. “We both agreed we aren’t looking for romance. We don’t want to muck up our partnership with unwanted emotions.”

Unwanted. He was being rejected before he’d even had a chance to tell her that he did want to explore what was going on between them. He should have known better. His judgment was way off when it came to women. Maybe even to all other aspects of his life.

The reflection of the sun off a windshield caught his attention. He watched what was happening behind them for a moment and his chest tightened for a different reason.

“We have a tail,” he said, his gaze still on the rearview mirror. “A nondescript silver sedan four cars back. It’s been with us since we left Denver.”

Maren sat forward again and leaned to her right to look at the passenger side-view mirror. “I see it. But are you sure? The traffic’s so heavy.”

He wasn’t sure. He wasn’t sure of anything at the moment. Wasn’t sure he could trust his judgment. With the way she’d kissed him back yesterday, he’d thought she was feeling the same attraction and affection that was crowding his own chest. But apparently not. “Let’s just keep an eye on the car.”

For the rest of the drive to Boulder they remained silent. The silver sedan dropped back another few cars. But it kept pace with them. When he took the exit for Boulder city center, the sedan passed the exit.

He breathed out a relieved sigh.

“Can you fire up your GPS on that burner phone and get us to Boulder Memorial Hospital?”

Maren took out the phone Colt had given her and found the directions. When they arrived at the hospital, he parked in a spot designated for law enforcement.

After releasing the dogs and letting them have a few minutes on the lawn outside the entrance, the four of them walked into the hospital. For some reason the hairs at the nape of Colt’s neck quivered. He paused to glance back and saw a silver sedan slide into a parking place four rows from the exit. A dark-haired woman in a bright pink top and jeans emerged from the car, but she kept her face turned away from the entrance. She appeared harmless as she hitched her purse on her shoulder.

He gave his head a shake. He couldn’t be sure if it was the same make or model as the one he’d thought was following them. There were a lot of silver sedans out there. But with Shadow seeming to always be hovering close, he couldn’t dislodge the thought they had been followed.

Inside the hospital, he touched Maren's lower back, the gesture oddly natural.

She glanced at him with curiosity. "Something wrong?"

"Keep your head on a swivel," he said. "I don't know why, but I just have a bad feeling."

She nodded and tugged Haven closer to her side. "Always alert, always prepared."

He gave a wry chuckle. She was a feisty woman, and he really liked her. More than liked her. But he needed to hold his feelings for her in check. Because, obviously, she didn't feel the same.

Aware of the curious and interested stares aimed at the two dogs, Colt made sure his badge was visible. Maren did as well. At the information desk, they asked for Agent Spares's room number.

They were directed to the sixth floor, east wing, room 659.

When they arrived on the sixth floor, they stopped at the nurses' station to alert the staff they were there.

"Has he regained consciousness?" Maren asked the duty nurse.

"He has been in and out of consciousness," the nurse replied. "But he's very weak from blood loss."

"We'll only be a minute," Colt assured the woman.

They walked down the hall past rooms with beeping monitors and the low murmur of conversations and televisions, to find Agent Spares's room. The door was closed.

Colt frowned. "I would've thought there would be an agent on duty outside."

"Do you really think he's in danger?" Maren glanced up and down the hallway as if searching for any threats.

"I think Steve was the target. I'm sure that's what my boss thought, too," Colt said, assuring himself as much as her.

Still, if he'd been in charge, he would've posted somebody

outside the door. Spares was a DEA agent after all. He deserved respect and protection.

"Or we could have been the target," Maren murmured with a shiver.

Unable to deny that tidbit, he said, "True."

Colt knocked on the door then pushed it open. They entered the dimly lit room with the dogs at their heels. Agent Spares lay on a bed with the railings up on either side. A heart monitor and oxygen tubes were attached to him. His shoulder where he'd been hit by a bullet was wrapped in bandages. His eyes were closed. He was a thin man with dark, wispy hair and a thin mustache that stood out against the pastiness of his skin.

Colt reached out a hand and gently touched the man's uninjured shoulder. "Agent Spares. Henry."

Henry's eyes fluttered and then slowly opened. His dark eyes focused on Colt then widened.

Colt wasn't sure why he saw panic in the man's eyes. "You're okay. You're here in the hospital."

Henry's gaze focused on Maren as she moved to stand on the other side of the bed. Then narrowed with confusion. "Who are you?" he rasped out.

"Officer Maren Anderson with Colorado Springs PD," Maren said in a firm tone. "You said Steve Loren had information he would only give to me. What did he want to tell me?"

Henry shook his head, the confusion clearing. "He wouldn't say. Just kept insisting he needed to talk to the lady cop who looked like Opal. I had no idea what that meant." Henry's gaze turned back to Colt.

"They're twins," Colt told him.

Henry's eyes widened and then he nodded with realization. "That makes sense."

Colt met Maren's gaze across the bed.

Her gracefully arched brows came together. "Are you saying

Special Agent in Charge Herman didn't tell anyone that Opal was alive or that she has a twin?"

Colt wasn't sure what to make of this development. He'd informed his SAC the minute he'd realized he was dealing with twins.

Henry shrugged, then winced. "He didn't tell me. But I'm the low man on the organizational chart. Only been with the agency for less than a year."

Still, Colt thought it odd that his SAC, Leo, hadn't informed the agents watching over Steve Loren of this detail.

Could Leo be involved with Shadow? Could that be how Shadow was constantly one step ahead of the agency's efforts to bring him down?

The suspicion caused a riot of anxiety and acute agitation to camp out in his chest. He hated to think the boss was dirty.

"I'm sorry I couldn't be more helpful," Henry said. "I'm sorry about your sister."

"Thank you," Maren said. Her voice held a curious note to it. "Have you met my sister?"

"Only know of her by reputation," Henry said.

"Can you explain why you told us to come through the front door?" Colt asked, still puzzling out the odd request.

Making a face filled with pain, Henry said, "Sorry. My head is fuzzy. I don't recall saying that."

"You don't?" Colt and Maren shared a look of disbelief.

Henry shook his head on a wince. His eyelids fluttered closed. "No."

Figuring they wouldn't be getting any more information out of him at the moment, Colt said, "We'll let you get some rest." He gestured to Maren with his head toward the door.

She nodded. "If you think of anything Steve might've said that could help us find Opal, I would appreciate if you let us know."

Henry's head bobbed, though his eyes remained closed. "Of course. Anything I can do to help."

Leaving the room without any more information than what they'd entered with, Colt swallowed down his frustration. Actually, they had learned something. For some reason his SAC had withheld information from the other agents. Why? Colt was determined to find out.

"Excuse me." A tall, gray-haired man in a white lab coat with a name tag identifying him as Dr. Benjamin Sweeney stopped them. "I understand you're visiting Agent Spares."

"We were," Colt said showing the man his badge. Maren did the same.

The doctor glanced around, then drew them off to the side, away from the nurses' station and into an alcove. Lowering his voice, he said, "There's something strange about the agent's wound. I've been debating whether I should say anything or not. But I think you should know."

Dread and anticipation had Colt frowning. "Tell us. We're here to help."

The doctor looked about again to make sure no one was within earshot. "His wound isn't fresh. It's at least a few days old. He wasn't treated after it initially happened, and that's why he had so much blood loss. And the wound had time to become infected."

Beside Colt, Maren let out a small gasp of surprise.

Stunned himself, Colt contemplated the ramifications of this news. Three days ago, he'd shot a masked man who tried to kill Maren. Was Agent Henry Spares that man? Was Henry the man known as Shadow? Or only working for him? Was that why he'd conveniently forgotten about telling them to come in the front door of the safe house when he seemed to clearly remember other details very well? Something was off with the guy.

"Doctor, please keep this to yourself for now," Maren said

in a take-charge voice. To Colt she said, "We need to go back and talk to Agent Spares. He could be in league with Shadow."

"My thought exactly." Colt appreciated that he and Maren were of the same mind. He really liked this woman.

They hurried back down the hall toward room 659.

A female nurse, covered from head to toe in green scrubs and a matching scrub hat and mask, slipped out of Spares's room.

"Hey, stop," Colt called. That bad feeling he'd had earlier amplified.

The nurse picked up her pace and disappeared out of sight.

Seconds later, a loud, shrill beeping emanated from Agent Spares's room.

Maren bolted into the room ahead of Colt.

On the hospital bed, Henry's body was convulsing, his eyes rolling back in his head.

"Get help! I'm going after the nurse," Maren yelled. And sprinted out of the room, with Haven at her side.

He didn't have to make the call as hospital personnel pushed past him and Rusk, rushing to the bed. For ten minutes the medical staff worked on Henry, but in the end the man expired.

Dr. Sweeney called time of death.

"What happened?" Colt said to the doctor. "Did that nurse give him something?"

"I won't know until we can fully examine the body," Dr. Sweeney told him. "But this wasn't a natural occurrence. I would stake my professional reputation on it."

Dread and anger surged through Colt.

Agent Henry Spares, who Colt might have shot a few days ago, had been murdered.

Maren and Haven took the stairs all the way to the exit that came out on the side of the hospital. With Haven sniffing the air, Maren searched for the nurse. But since she'd only gotten a glimpse of the person dressed in scrubs, she couldn't be sure who of the hospital personnel or civilians walking around was the culprit.

A squeal of tires snapped her attention to a silver sedan racing out of the parking lot. Her stomach dropped. They *had* been followed. And whoever was in that car had just been in Agent Spares's room. What had they done to the man?

She headed back up to the sixth floor to find Colt talking with the hospital security.

"Agents Spares?" she asked as she approached.

The anger creating brackets around Colt's mouth alerted her to the answer before he said, "Dead."

Grief for a life cut short stabbed at her. "I lost the nurse. She left in a silver sedan."

Something flashed in Colt's eyes. "I saw a woman get out of a silver sedan when we came in. Maybe we can identify her." He gestured to the security guards. "They're going to let us see the hospital security footage."

They followed the two officers to a control room where a bank of monitors was set up. An officer sat in front of the computer screens and pointed to a twenty-seven-inch monitor to his right. He scrolled backward, showing Maren and Colt entering Agent Spares's room and leaving. Then, seconds later, the nurse entered the room and was in there for less than thirty seconds before slipping out just as Maren and Colt headed back to the room.

"Do you have cameras in the stairwells?" Maren asked.

"This one," the officer said, gesturing to another screen. "We can see the person rushing down and exiting the building." He pointed to another camera. "We can track the nurse to the parking lot. Then she ducked down between two large vehicles. No one else appears until you step out of the exit."

"A silver sedan left the parking lot maybe a minute later," Maren said. "Can you get a license on it?"

The officer scrolled forward showing the sedan leaving the spot and going out the exit. The license plate was missing.

Fisting her hands, Maren looked at Colt. "We need to talk to your SAC."

He nodded, though the expression in his eyes was grim.

Colt had his gaze on the parking lot monitor. "Wait a second. Can you zero in on that blue van parked near the exit under the shade of that tree?"

The officer enlarged the photo to show a blue panel van. They could see that there was somebody sitting in the driver seat, but the visor was down, and the person's face hidden.

"Is that—" Maren couldn't believe it. The same panel van that had run her off the road. "But didn't it burn?"

"Agent Spares was the one who told us that." Colt's voice reverberated with anger. "Looks like he was definitely dirty."

"We need to get down to that van and see who's driving."

Even as the words left her mouth, the van pulled out of the parking spot and exited the parking lot, disappearing out of view. It too was without a license plate.

"This is not good," Colt said. "One of our own was dirty. Maybe more agents are involved. I don't know how high up this will go. Could Leo be on the take?"

The horror on Colt's face combined with the thought of the DEA SAC in league with drug dealers stole Maren's breath. "It could be how Shadow has managed to evade the DEA for so long. I'll call Emmett and let him know what's happening," Maren said as she left the security office.

Colt was right behind her. "Can you hold off on that until I talk to SAC Herman?" Colt asked. "Leo's been my boss the whole time I've been with the DEA. I can't believe he's in on this." He winced. "I don't want to believe it. I have to give him the benefit of the doubt. Give him a chance to defend himself."

She stared at him, wondering if his judgment could be trusted. Even as the thought formed, she dismissed it. She trusted Colt. And she owed him this opportunity. Still, her loyalty was to the task force. “Let’s head back to Denver. You can talk to your SAC, but I do have to tell Emmett. I’m sorry, but my allegiance is with the Colorado K-9 Unit.”

Colt heaved a sigh and nodded. “I understand. And I would be the same way if the circumstances were reversed.”

She was glad he understood, but she couldn’t help feeling like whatever answers they discovered were going to hurt.

SEVENTEEN

When they arrived at the Rocky Mountain division offices of the DEA agency, Colt brought the SUV to a halt. A conflagration of emotions whirred within him. He was about to accuse his boss of colluding with, if not actually being, Shadow. Nausea rolled through him.

He turned to Maren. "I should do this alone."

Her pretty eyes were sympathetic. "No way. We're partners," she said. "And for now, you're part of the Colorado K-9 Unit task force as well. Where you go, I go."

He appreciated her determination and her support. "I don't know if he'll talk to me with you there."

"Colt, I know this is going to be hard." She put a hand on his arm, her touch warm and solid. "But we do this together."

Considering he wasn't sure he could trust his own judgment, he nodded.

They retrieved the dogs from the back and headed into the agency. They passed through the metal detectors, showed their IDs and then took the elevator to the top floor, where the SAC's office was located. Through the glass panel next to the door, Colt saw the Special Agent in Charge Leo Herman sitting at his desk talking to someone out of view. Leo was in his late sixties, tough as nails, with a buzz cut of gray hair and a square build. As a young man he'd been a marine, and had the same mentality in the DEA.

Despite the turmoil going on inside his gut, Colt knocked. And met Leo's gaze through the window. Leo waved him in.

Colt opened the door so he and Maren could step inside with the dogs. Surprise arced through Colt to find Agent Daniel Russell sitting in a chair. Unlike the last time they'd seen Daniel, he was now dressed in a dark gray charcoal business suit with a red tie. He had one ankle crossed over his knee. His hair was perfectly groomed and his face clean-shaven.

"Your ears must have been ringing," Daniel said as Colt shut the door behind him.

Colt wasn't sure whom he was addressing, but chose to ignore the comment and focus on Leo, his boss. "Can we speak? Privately."

Leo's eyebrows rose. "Anything you say to me can be said to the new deputy special agent in charge," Leo said.

Stunned, Colt's gaze jumped back to Daniel. "I didn't know you were up for the position. Congratulations."

Daniel gave an imperious nod. "I was surprised you didn't put your hat in the ring for the job."

"I've been busy." Colt's single-minded focus on bringing down Shadow hadn't allowed him to consider the promotion. The quest for justice and the determination to take the poison off the streets had taken over his life, making him miss family gatherings and giving him no time for much else, including job growth.

Leo stood, his gaze on Maren. "I'm sorry, we haven't been introduced," he said.

She stepped forward to shake his hand. "Officer Maren Anderson, Colorado Springs PD and the Colorado K-9 Unit task force."

Leo nodded. "I've spoken with your team leader, Special Agent Emmett Dane." He flicked a glance at Colt. "I was surprised when he requested for you to be temporarily assigned to the task force."

"Colt has been a valuable asset to our efforts to bring down a baby smuggling ring. And I'm helping him take down the drug trafficker known as Shadow," Maren said with pride in her voice that sent warmth through Colt's chest.

"As well as find your missing sister," Daniel piped in.

Both Maren and Colt turned their gazes to the agent.

"Do you have a lead on my sister?" Maren asked.

Daniel held up his hands. "No, we don't. I think any relevant information died with Colt's CI."

Colt glanced at Maren just as she glanced at him. By silent agreement they both kept quiet about Vinnie Homer. Though Colt was certain he'd already mentioned the man to Daniel a couple days ago. Why was he pretending not to have heard?

Had he and Maren just walked into a den of vipers?

Colt turned to Leo. "Agent Spares was murdered. The suspect is at large."

The shock on Leo's face couldn't have been faked. "When did this happen?"

Daniel jumped to his feet. "I knew we should have put an officer at the door."

Leo turned to Daniel and snapped, "You said he wasn't the target. That Steve Loren was. Why would somebody kill Henry?"

Confused and conflicted, Colt said, "That's the million-dollar question. Henry claimed that Steve wouldn't give him the information that he had wanted to tell Maren. But maybe Steve did tell Henry before being shot."

"Agent Spares also lied to us," Maren said. "He claimed that the blue panel van that ran me off the road was found burned. But we saw it on the parking lot security camera at the hospital."

Daniel swore. "I didn't know. Henry had to be part of Shadow's network of spies."

"The doctor tending to Henry informed us Henry's wound

was old and infected," Colt said, watching both men carefully for their reactions to the news.

Leo tucked in his chin. "How can that be?"

Daniel's eyebrows drew together. "What?"

"I winged one of the masked men who tried to kill Officer Anderson a few days ago," Colt said.

Leo looked like he was going to be sick. He ran a hand over his bristled hair and sat back down. "This has to stay between the four of us. If word gets out that we know Agent Spares was dirty, whoever his accomplices are might go underground." He turned his sharp-eyed gaze to Colt. "I've tried to keep your progress quiet after you informed me that your CI claimed Shadow had informants in all branches of law enforcement."

Colt wanted to believe him, but he wasn't sure whom to trust. "We're due at the Colorado K-9 Unit headquarters." Though technically not true, they needed to meet with Emmett and get his take on the situation.

Colt was going to need the task force now more than ever to bring down Shadow. But would Emmett do as he promised and provide the resources they needed? Or would taking down Shadow have to wait until they could find Mia and break up this baby smuggling ring? Time was running out to find Opal and to seize their chance to arrest Shadow.

"I've known Special Agent in Charge Leo Herman for a very long time." Emmett stood behind his desk. "There is no way that man is corrupt. I would stake my reputation and my life on it."

Hearing her boss vouch for Colt's boss had Maren tied up in knots. She knew how upset Colt had been when they'd left the DEA offices, thinking that his boss was dirty. They'd gone there to confront him but had ended up leaving without any answers.

She'd been pleasantly surprised by Colt's insistence they talk to Emmett because her boss was a man of honor and integrity, and she believed he would be a voice of reason. When they arrived at the task force headquarters, they'd taken the dogs to the training center for a much-needed break with water and some exercise. Then they'd headed upstairs to talk to Emmett.

Beside her, Colt shifted his weight. He had his arms crossed over his chest and his feet braced apart. "How can you be sure?"

"You're just going to have to trust me," Emmett said.

"I'm sorry to say right now that trust is in short supply," Colt said.

Maren turned to Colt and put a hand on his shoulder. "We do know that Agent Spares was somehow involved with Shadow. That's a lead we can follow."

Colt held her gaze. She saw his upset swirling in his gorgeous green eyes and wanted to comfort him, but at the moment, the best she could do was to give his shoulder a squeeze.

"You're right, of course," Colt said. Still his body vibrated with tension. She could feel the tightness beneath her palm.

"Go see Eva," Emmett said. "Have her dig into this agent's life. He certainly wasn't doing it for fame or glory. There has to be a money trail to follow."

"Thank you, Emmett," Maren said. She tugged Colt with her out of her boss's office.

"I know you don't want to believe this and aren't ready to trust Emmett, but he is one of the good guys," Maren told him. "I wouldn't have joined his task force if I thought otherwise."

Colt ran a hand through his hair as they made their way to Eva's office. "I trust your judgment more than my own."

Though she was glad to hear he trusted her, she didn't like him disparaging himself. "Colt, you are a great agent. You have good instincts. You knew something was wrong at the hospital before anything happened. We need to trust your gut."

His expression said loud and clear that he wasn't buying it. She didn't know how to get him to believe in himself. But she felt compelled to try. "You have to forgive yourself for not seeing through Rebecca."

"I don't know..." he said with a shake of his head.

She took his hand. "Listen to me, you are not to blame for her deception. If our situations were reversed, you'd be telling me the same thing."

A softening in his gaze had her heart pounding.

"You're right," he said, his voice tender. "And so wise."

A flutter of something she didn't want to analyze had her releasing her hold on him. "Let's go talk to Eva." She needed to stay focused on the task as hand.

They found Eva at her desk. She was more than willing to dig into Henry's financials. "It might take me a while. Since he's in law enforcement, he would know how to hide his money."

"How long?" Colt asked, impatience threading through his voice.

Eva considered then said, "Give me two hours."

"That will allow us time to get some food," Maren said. They hadn't eaten since leaving the ranch several hours earlier. And Colt needed a break—though he tried to hide his anxiousness, she knew he was stressed. So was she. They needed fuel to unravel this mystery and deal with everything that came next.

They headed to the cafeteria in the building. Maren chose a chef's salad and Colt grabbed a ham and cheese sandwich. After unwrapping the plastic from around the two halves, he left the sandwich untouched.

"You need to eat," she said, stabbing a fork into her salad. "You won't be worth anything if your blood sugar tanks. Or you're walking around hangry."

His eyebrow arched and his mouth tipped up at the corner in a way that made her heart do a funny bump. "I think your concern is based on self-preservation."

She smiled across the table at him. "True. But also, I care about you." And the truth in the words wouldn't be denied. She more than cared, but at the moment that was all she was willing to admit.

His eyebrows rose. “Really? I had the feeling you wanted to keep me at an emotional distance.”

She grimaced, realizing he was referring to their conversation in the SUV earlier. What she’d told him was true. They both had agreed they weren’t looking for romance and she didn’t want to mess with their partnership. However, she hadn’t told him everything. Like the fact she was fighting to keep her emotions in check. She was falling for him big-time. But she didn’t want growing attachment to impair either of their judgments or their professional work ethics. So instead, she teased, “Is someone feeling sorry for themselves?”

He made a face and took a big bite of the sandwich.

Colt’s phone buzzed, then rang. He looked at the caller ID. His audible intake of breath caught as he glanced up at Maren. “The US Marshals.”

A mix of hope and concern dropped into Maren’s stomach, and she set down her fork, pushing the rest of her lunch away.

Colt put the phone on speaker and turned the volume to low. “Colt here. I’m with Officer Maren Anderson. What news do you have?”

“Hello, Colt. Hello, Maren. This is Deputy Walker McCane with the Denver Marshals office. I wanted to let you know our protectee, Vinnie Homer, received a text from Opal Anderson with information for where to meet her.”

Maren grabbed a napkin and a pen from her backpack and wrote down the information as Walker gave it. “Can we trust Vinnie?”

“That, I’m not sure,” Walker said. “The guy’s still detoxing. If given half a chance he’d rabbit.”

Maren remembered how desperate Vinnie had been for a fix, and he would run away like a scared rabbit if the marshals weren’t careful. “You can’t let that happen.”

“He needs to stay clean,” Colt added. “We can’t lose another person to these drugs.”

"We're doing our best," the marshal said.

"Thank you, we appreciate the info," Maren said and pushed the end button on Colt's phone. "Let's go."

"Not so fast," Colt said, holding up a hand. "What if this is a setup? What if Shadow got to him somehow?"

"That's the chance we have to take to find Opal," she said. There was no way she was letting an opportunity to find her sister pass by.

"I understand and admire your determination," Colt said. "But I don't like the situation. We have no way of knowing what we will be walking into. It could be a trap. Shadow has to be aware by now that you're not Opal."

Maren weighed his words. "The risk is worth it to me."

"We'll need reinforcements." Colt sent off a text to Emmett, alerting the task force leader to what was happening.

Colt's phone dinged with an incoming text. He glanced at it. "I was expecting a reply from Emmett, but this looks like a text message from Walker."

Maren's heart lodged in her throat. Had something happened to Opal? "Read it."

"It says, 'This is a text from Opal on Vinnie's phone that I'm forwarding.' Below, the forwarded text reads, 'Tell the jumping bean I can't wait to see her.'"

Tears misted in Maren's eyes. "That's Opal's childhood nickname for me."

"Because of the gymnastics," Colt said.

She gave him a watery smile. "You remembered."

"Yes." His green gaze bore into her. "I have a feeling I'll remember everything about my time with you."

His words settled over her like a cozy blanket. As much as she wanted to reciprocate the sentiment, she couldn't. Not now. Not when she was close to finding her sister. That had to take priority. But she didn't look forward to the day when she and Colt separated and went their own ways.

* * *

Despite his misgivings, Colt accepted the body armor from Emmett. After informing the task force leader that they had heard from the US Marshals and there was a meet set up with Opal in Pike-San Isabel National Forest, Emmett had insisted that Colton and Maren gear up.

They'd headed straight for the task force's armory located in a large room adjacent to the training center, filled with various types and sizes of Kevlar vests, ammunition and weapons.

"Here, use these Bluetooth ear comms," Emmett said, handing both Colt and Maren a small box. "You'll have about a mile range. But be aware, in the forest, the service can be spotty."

Colt put the earpiece into his ear canal. "I'm still not sure this is a good idea."

Maren's gaze snapped to him as she strapped on a thin black bulletproof vest over the task force T-shirt she'd changed into earlier that day. He missed the flowing dress she'd worn at his parents' house and the way she'd let her hair cascade over her shoulders. Now, it was braided in a thick pleat.

"I told you I will do whatever is necessary to get my sister back," Maren stated, her tone firm. "Coming in with the full might of the task force would scare her. She would never trust anything I said if I came after her with a small army. It has to be just me."

"Not just you," Colt said, donning a Kevlar vest. "Where you go, I go."

"You can rest assured," Emmett said, "that the task force will be on standby. We won't be seen, but we will be in the vicinity."

That gave Colt a measure of comfort. He'd elected to call in the task force rather than the DEA because he wasn't sure if there were more moles within the agency.

But if this was a setup by Shadow, things could go south before backup arrived. He grabbed two extra 9 mm magazines and stuffed them into the pockets of his tactical cargo pants.

Seeing Maren struggle with the sleeve of her task force windbreaker, he moved to help her.

She jerked away. "I've got it."

He frowned and lifted his hands. "Just trying to be helpful."

Her face softened. "I'm sorry. It's just all the anxiety. What is Opal doing in the middle of a national forest? Has she been sleeping in the elements? What about the baby? Has she been eating? Does she have water?"

Aware of Emmett, Colt restrained himself from taking Maren into his arms. "Opal reached out. That has to be enough for now. All the questions will be answered in due time."

Holding his gaze, Maren nodded. "It's all so maddening."

He understood. The waiting, hoping and praying. Having to accept that sometimes God said no, or not right now, stretched a person's faith.

"Let's get the dogs and head out," he said, hoping if they were on the move maybe Maren would feel better.

She gave him a grateful smile. "That seems to be our MO, doesn't it?"

He gave her a half laugh. "Seems so."

After retrieving Rusk and Haven and securing them in the back compartment, he drove as fast as he dared to the trailhead on the edge of the national forest halfway between Denver and Colorado Springs, just outside the small town of Manitou Springs. The ultra-prominent Pikes Peak was one of the highest and most popular summits along the Rocky Mountains. At the base, timber stretched as far as the eye could see, climbing up the mountain and interspersed with craggy rocks and pink-hued, jutting formations of granite.

They left the SUV in the gravel parking lot and hiked on foot until they came to where the hiking trail veered to the left, heading up the mountain.

Maren surveyed the area and turned to Colt. "My sister has

to be somewhere on the valley floor. Give me at least a fifteen-minute head start before you follow."

They'd agreed on the way over that he would trail behind her and Haven. Making sure that they were within a mile's distance of each other so that they could be heard over the wireless comms.

She and Haven trekked into the forest off the trail.

Rusk whined and stared up at Colt.

He smoothed a hand over the dog's sleek head. "I know. We'll have their backs. Just from a distance."

He prayed that would be enough.

Maren and Haven picked their way through the underbrush, trying to discern any sort of path her sister might have taken. Haven's ears twitched and her body quivered as she strained at the lead, pulling Maren forward until they came to a small grove. Maren's breath caught and held in her chest. A small tent had been erected beneath the canopy of two trees that had grown into each other.

"Opal," Maren called out. There was no movement inside the tent.

"What did you find?" Colt's voice sounded in her ear.

In a low voice, Maren replied, "A tent. I'm going to approach and look inside."

With every fiber of her being, she braced herself. What if Opal was— No, she couldn't even let her mind go there. Her sister had to be alive. But she could be ill or injured. Maren decisively unzipped the tent and pulled the flap back. Inside was an empty sleeping bag, a half-used case of water and a stack of boxes filled with various kinds of protein bars. Where was her sister?

Feeling a tug on Haven's leash, Maren backed out of the tent to focus on the Doberman staring at a clump of trees.

"Opal, are you there?"

From the shadows, her sister emerged. She'd lost so much weight. Her hair, once the exact glossy honey brown as Maren's, was dirty and matted to her head. Her clothes, the army green jacket and black pants, were the same as what she'd worn the last time Maren had seen her in front of the Barren Valley Clinic. They hung on her slim frame and slightly rounded belly.

Every cell in Maren's body rebelled at the sight of her twin in such a state. And worry chomped through her over the pregnancy given all that Opal had been through while in hiding. Was the baby okay?

Her instinct was to rush to her sister, but caution had her moving slowly in case she startled Opal into running. Opal's gaze went to Haven, and she backed up a step, fear pinching her face. Halting to reel Haven to her side, she put the dog in a down position and dropped the lead. "Stay."

Confident Haven would obey, Maren proceeded forward until she was standing right in front of her sister.

"You came," Opal said, her voice barely audible.

"Of course, I came. I will always come for you," Maren said, emphasizing her words. "All you ever have to do, Opal, is call me."

Big tears welled in Opal's eyes. "I wasn't sure. I mean, I'm such a disappointment."

Groaning as her heart folded in on itself, Maren gathered her sister into her arms. "You are not a disappointment. I am so sorry I wasn't a better sister. I was too caught up in my own grief and anger to notice how you were spiraling. By the time I had the wherewithal to pay attention—you were gone."

Opal's arms came around Maren, squeezing tight. "You're here now."

Feeling the baby bump, Maren pulled back. "Are you and the baby well?"

Opal put a hand on her tummy. "I think so. I ran out of my vitamins, though."

"We'll get you more and seen by a reputable doctor," Maren assured her. From now on, Maren would protect both Opal and the baby.

A deep growl came from Haven.

Maren twisted to look behind her. The dog was still in the down position, but her ears were pricked upward, and her teeth were bared in a snarl. But the dog wasn't looking at Maren and Opal. She was focused away from them, toward the trees.

She was alerting to danger.

Heart jackknifing in her chest, Maren said, "Come." Haven jumped up and ran to her side. To Opal she said, "We have to get to safety."

They'd taken three steps toward the concealment of the forest when gunfire rang out. Bullets whizzed through the air, slamming into the trees. Maren grabbed Opal and pulled her to the ground, covering her body with hers. Haven barked, furiously. "Down."

Haven dropped to her belly beside Maren's prone body.

In her ear, she heard Colt saying, "Maren, what's happening?"

"Taking gunfire," she said. To Opal, she said, "We have to make a break for it. We're sitting ducks out here."

Crouched, they ran for the safety of the trees as bullets peppered the ground around them, whizzing past their heads. Maren took them in a zigzag line. Why were they missing? Were the shooters trying to push them farther into the forest? Maren and Opal scrambled behind the trunk of a thick tree.

Opal's face twisted with horror. "Are you working with Shadow?"

Aghast that her sister would even contemplate such a horrible thing, Maren could only stare. "Opal, why would you think that?!"

"Then who are you talking to?"

"My partner," she told her sister.

In her ear, Colt said, “We’re coming.”

Then Emmett’s voice also sounded in her ear. “On our way.”

“Hurry.” Maren withdrew her weapon and shot toward the trees where the shooter seemed to be located.

Haven gave another loud, warning bark.

Maren turned in time to see Opal running away and disappearing into the thick forest.

“Opal!” Maren screamed and took off after her sister.

EIGHTEEN

Fear slid along Colt's limbs. He couldn't hear anything coming from Maren's comms. Running with Rusk at his heels for all they were worth, they came out through the trees to a small clearing where he found Opal's campsite. The sound of more gunfire burst through the forest.

He swiveled toward the noise. Believing the gunfire came from the north, Colt and his K-9 took off in that direction into the forest.

When the gunfire ceased, Colt skidded to a halt, realizing he had no idea which direction to go. Where had Maren and her sister run off to? Back toward the road? Up the mountain toward the summit? East, west, north or south?

"I lost them," Colt said, unable to keep the despair from his voice.

"We're almost to the coordinates. Meet us there," Emmett said, referring to the location of Opal's campsite.

Heart in his throat, he and Rusk backtracked to the makeshift campsite, but he couldn't reverse the fear crowding his mind.

Maren caught a glimpse of Opal up ahead and pushed herself to move faster, using every bit of energy she possessed to gain on her twin. Finally, she caught up to Opal, who had slowed and was wheezing slightly.

Maren grabbed the back of Opal's army green jacket and pulled her behind a fallen pine tree.

Opal gasped and clutched at her chest. "You scared me."

"What are you thinking?" Maren said. Anger and fear and frustration vibrated in her voice and throughout her body. Haven moved closer to Maren. "You could have been killed."

"You were followed," Opal accused. "How do I know you're not in league with them?"

Reining in her upset and taking deep, calming breaths, Maren gentled herself enough to say, "Opal, I'm on your side." She put a hand on Haven and could feel the tension in her body. "I don't know how I was followed. But I need you to know I will not let anything happen to you. You must trust me."

"I do," Opal said. The fight drained from her and her whole body slumped onto the ground. She drew her knees up to her chest and put her forehead on her folded arms. "I'm so tired."

Sympathy and empathy grabbed a hold of Maren, and she gathered her sister in her arms. "I've got you." Needing to know what Opal knew, Maren said, "I understand you can identify Shadow."

Opal lifted her head and met Maren's gaze. There was sorrow in her blue eyes. "Georgy warned me to stay hidden while he told Shadow we wanted out. But I had to see what was happening. And then Shadow shot Georgy and I screamed. I know Shadow saw me. I ran and managed to escape."

"Can you describe him?"

"Yeah. Thin, dark-haired, dark mustache. Weaselly," she said with a shudder.

Maren recognized the description. "That sounds like Agent Henry Spares. You don't have to worry. He's dead."

Though the mystery remained of who killed him and why. Was it simply a matter of cutting off the head of the snake and a new one growing back?

"He's only part of Shadow," Opal said, her voice sounding weak.

Putting her hand on her arm, Maren asked around the trepidation clawing up her chest, "What do you mean?"

"He has a partner. I don't know who. But I do know there's someone else. At least, Georgy was sure of it. My Georgy was smart. We were going to get out of the life. Run and take our baby as far away as we could." Tears slipped down her face.

Maren's heart bumped against her rib cage. "Why didn't you contact me? I could've helped you both."

A spasm of grief and pain marred Opal's face. "I didn't know if I could trust you."

Heart sinking, Maren pressed her lips together.

"I'm sorry, Maren," Opal said. "I should've known better. But it had been so long and there's been so much—"

The sound of pounding feet running toward them had Maren tensing and Haven growling. The Doberman moved to stand in front of Maren.

"Stay down," she ordered her sister as well as her dog. For extra measure, she gave Haven the down gesture. Slowly, as if reluctantly, the K-9 folded into the down position.

Withdrawing her weapon, Maren rose to peer over a fallen log. Her eyebrows rose as Agent Daniel Russell came into view. He skidded to a halt as his gaze met hers.

He lifted his hands, pointing his weapon up into the air. "Whoa, whoa. Colt called for backup."

"Where'd you come from?" Maren asked. She'd thought he'd decided against involving the DEA. But he had told his boss. Maybe the SAC had sent Daniel.

"The fire road." He pointed behind him.

Hesitation kept Maren in place. She holstered her gun. "I need to let Colt know." She'd long lost the Bluetooth signal connecting her to Colt. She reached for her cell phone.

Daniel beat her to it. Taking his phone out and dialing, he said, "I'll call him."

Maren helped her sister to stand. Haven rose, her ears twitching, and her dark eyes trained on Daniel.

"Who's that?" Suspicion and fear laced Opal's voice.

"He works with my partner," Maren told her. "They're DEA."

Opal jerked away from Maren. "You did sell me out."

Outraged, Maren stared. "No. They've been helping me find you. I'm helping them to bring down Shadow and his organization."

Still wary, Opal allowed Maren to lead her to where Daniel was talking to Colt. Haven stuck close to her side.

"I've got the women," Daniel said into the phone. "We'll meet you. I'll get them there."

Maren reached toward the phone. "I want to talk to him."

Daniel made a face as he put his phone back in his pocket. "Sorry, he already hung up."

Wondering how far away Colt and the team were, she asked, "Where are we going to meet?"

"The trailhead," Daniel said. "This way. I've a SUV on the fire road."

Daniel turned and marched forward. Maren narrowed her gaze on his back. The arrogant man thought she would just follow without question. Keeping her guard up, she hoped that letting him lead her and Opal out of the forest to the fire road would bring the comms back in range so she could communicate with Colt and the task force.

She took Opal by the arm, and they moved to follow the agent.

Rusk alerted before Colt even heard the sound of people descending onto the campsite. Surprise arced through him. It was the whole team. They'd all come.

Each was dressed in tactical gear and the K-9s wore their vests.

Emmett and his Newfoundland, Gemma, moved forward while the others hung back, awaiting orders.

"Is she on comms?" Emmett asked.

Colt shook his head, frustration making his blood boil. "She's out of range."

"We'll find her," Emmett said confidently. He studied the ground and moved southeast, away from the campsite. "There's broken grass over here as if people had run through here. I'm guessing this must be the way the twins went."

Colt berated himself. He'd gone north toward the sound of gunfire rather than southeast as indicated by the trail in the grass. His and Rusk's training wasn't in wilderness tracking. But rather in urban settings looking for narcotics.

"You and I will go together," Emmett said. To the others he said, "Fan out and stay in pairs. Keep your radios on but silent."

The team members dispersed, pairing off and going in various directions.

As Colt and Emmett, with their K-9 partners, headed in the direction that Emmett thought Maren and her sister might have gone, Emmett said, "Eva wanted me to give you a message. She found a bank account in the Caymans belonging to Agent Henry Spares. But there's another name on the account."

"That makes sense," Colt said. "Someone killed him. Must be the person on the account with him. What's the name?"

"Agent Daniel Russell."

As the trees thinned close to the fire road, Maren glimpsed a blue vehicle beneath the shade of a tree. Her heart seized. It was the blue panel van.

Panic fluttered in her chest.

Trying not to let on that she'd noticed the vehicle, she purposely stumbled while unhooking the strap on her sidearm. Haven nudged her as if to try to keep her upright.

"Maren, you okay?" Opal said as she too stumbled.

"Yeah." As she straightened, Maren withdrew her weapon. Her gaze zeroed in on Daniel, who had halted and turned toward them, his weapon aimed at Opal.

Haven emitted a low growl.

"Oh no, you don't," Daniel said. "Drop the weapon. Unless you're okay with your sister taking a bullet between the eyes. Killing both her and the unborn child of my late lieutenant Georgy Trevino."

The horror of revelation dawned on Maren. "You're the other half of the duo known as Shadow."

Daniel scoffed. "Figure that out on your own, did you?"

"Kind of hard not to with a gun aimed at us." Maren tucked Opal behind her. Her sister sobbed softly. Maren reeled in the lead, keeping Haven close.

Daniel grinned. "So loyal to your sister. Doesn't matter. You're both going to die."

Beside Maren, Haven snarled at Daniel.

"Keep your dog in check or that's where the first bullet will go." Daniel swung the barrel of his Glock toward Haven.

Rage swept through Maren. "You shoot my dog, and I'll shoot you."

"Look around," Daniel said with a sweep of his free hand. "You're outmanned and outgunned."

Maren looked around and saw four armed people step out of the woods. Three men and one dark-haired woman. No doubt the nurse from the hospital who'd killed Henry. All had automatic weapons or handguns aimed at her and Opal.

"You'll never get away with this," Maren said as she laid her weapon on the ground at her feet. Beside her, Haven tensed and strained at the tight hold she had on the leash, keeping the Doberman from lunging at Daniel. "Colt and the task force that

I'm a part of will never rest until they find out who you are and bring you down."

"I have no doubt that they will search. But now that I have the new role of deputy special agent in charge, I'll have more power. I'll send Colt far away."

"Your boss won't allow that," Maren stated. At least she hoped Special Agent in Charge Herman wouldn't agree to Colt being removed from the case and from the state.

"I have Leo wrapped around my finger," Daniel boasted arrogantly. "Don't you know? I'm the Golden Boy. He'll do anything I say."

Remembering how Leo had said Daniel was the one to suggest they didn't need a guard outside Henry's room, she believed him.

In her ear, she heard Colt's voice, "Maren, we're close. Keep him talking."

Relief and hope bubbled up along with another emotion, bringing tears to the back of her eyes. She'd never been so glad to hear anyone's voice in her whole life. And it wasn't just because he was saving her and her sister from certain death, but because she loved him. Truly and deeply. And was willing to risk her heart for him.

She blinked up at Daniel, hating that a tear slipped down her cheek.

He cocked his head. "I didn't take you for a crier."

Opal shifted, leaning into Maren, drawing her attention. Her sister's pale face didn't bode well. She looked ready to faint at any moment. Wrapping an arm around Opal, Maren asked, "How did you and Henry get away with all that you've done?"

"It was easy," he said. "We would take shifts being Shadow while the other led law enforcement on a merry chase."

Maren's gaze searched the forest beyond the henchmen, hoping for a sign Colt and Emmett were closing in. "I'm sure I'll regret asking this, but why?"

Daniel tucked his chin and gave her a look that said, *Seriously?* "Why do you think? Money, of course. You think a man like me can live on the salary of a DEA agent?"

"Why become a DEA agent in the first place?"

He shrugged. "There was a time when I thought I could make a difference, but that's a fantasy. So why not profit off the activities of others?"

Burning questions rose to the surface and she had to ask, "Are you in league with the baby smuggling ring operating through Colorado? Do you know Dr. Derek Rolls? Do you know where Mia is?"

He arched an eyebrow. "I know that's why the task force was formed. But my organization has nothing to do with any of that business. And if I had any information, I would give it to you." His brow creased. "I really would, but alas, even if I had information, you wouldn't be alive to do anything with it." He gestured with the gun. "Let's get moving."

Noise off to the side in the trees had everyone turning as Colt and Rusk rushed into the clearing. The pair skidded to a halt. Rusk barked frantically. Haven joined in. Both dogs focused their attention on Daniel.

Maren's heart leaped into her throat. She sent up a prayer that somehow all of them would get out of this alive.

Terrified by the sight of Maren and her sister surrounded by gunmen, Colt holstered his weapon and held up his hands. He couldn't let anything happen to the twins. To Maren. She'd become his world. But right now he needed to buy time for the other task force members to find them. "Daniel, you don't have to do this. You can walk away. We won't say anything. You need to let Maren and Opal go."

He heard Maren's small gasp. Didn't she know by now he would do anything for her? He hoped she saw the gesture for what it was.

A declaration.

He loved Maren with all his heart. And he would gladly give up his mission for her, if that was what it took. He'd give up his badge and his life to protect her.

But they weren't out of the woods yet. Daniel had his finger on the trigger and the barrel of his gun was aimed at Maren's forehead. The sight so enraged Colt that he had to use every ounce of energy to keep from launching himself at the man and throttling him.

"I'm surprised it took you this long to get here," Daniel said. "I knew you were following her. My people have been following you."

The hairs on Colt's arm rose. Were there more gunmen?

Daniel gestured with his weapon. "Stand by your girlfriend and her loser of a sister. You'll want to die together."

He moved to stand next to Maren and met her gaze. "I'm sorry I didn't get here sooner. I lost the connection through our comms."

"I'm sorry! I took off without making sure you were within range."

"Stop your blathering," Daniel said. "I know the perfect place for the five of you to go off a cliff."

Colt's blood turned to ice. The man was truly deranged to want to kill the dogs. Daniel must not know about the baby Opal carried. Or didn't the man just not care?

Ignoring him, Colt continued to hold Maren's gaze. "We'll do what we have to."

"By any means necessary," she finished. Her gaze pointed at the leash in his hand and then to the ground.

He didn't need to be a mind reader to understand. He inclined his head slightly to indicate he understood her intent.

They both dropped the leads on their K-9s at the same time. Exchanging a subtle nod, they shouted at the same time, "Attack."

Confident that the dogs would do as instructed, Colt launched himself at Maren and Opal, taking them to the ground just as Daniel fired the gun. The bullet hit Colt smack in the back.

All around them, chaos ensued as the task force members and their K-9 partners erupted from the forest, the dogs barking as the team members took down the gunmen.

Daniel screamed as Haven's teeth sank into his forearm, forcing him to release the gun and driving him to his knees. Rusk jumped on his back, pushing him to the ground, and latched on to the back of Daniel's shirt, shaking his head back and forth.

"Out," Maren shouted. Haven released but Rusk continued to growl and shake his head.

Rolling to his back, Colt struggled to catch his breath from the impact of the bullet against his flak vest. He may have broken ribs, but at least they were all alive. But he couldn't find his voice to tell Rusk to let the man go.

Then Maren was on her knees to him, holding his face in her hands.

"Rusk," he managed in a faint voice.

Maren swiveled. "Rusk! Out! Come!"

Then the dog released his hold on Daniel's shirt, turned and ran to Colt's side. He plopped down on his belly and licked Colt's hand.

Maren's beautiful, tear-filled eyes stared at him with concern shining in their depths. "Please tell me the bullet didn't penetrate the vest."

Unable to speak yet, he shook his to indicate it hadn't.

She dropped her chin to her chest, her relief obvious.

Testing an inhale, he hissed air at the sharp pain in his upper left shoulder area.

Her gaze snapped back to his. "Take it easy."

"I know him," Opal groused, standing over Colt. "He's arrested me a few times. He's your partner?"

"Yes. Yes, he's my partner," Maren said with a soft smile and then she kissed him.

If only Colt had strength enough to kiss her back, he would. But his heart expanded, causing more pain in his rib cage.

Sirens filled the air. Maren helped Colt to a sitting position, and he was finally able to breathe fully. The sight around gave him grim pleasure. The gunmen who had been surrounding Maren and Opal were on their knees, with their hands cuffed behind them. Two additional men were also in custody. Apparently, Daniel did have additional gunmen.

Daniel was on his knees with his hands behind his back. Pain and rage etched lines on his face.

Colt took grim satisfaction in the sight.

"Maren..." Emmett drew their attention. "There's an ambulance here to take your sister to the hospital and have her checked out. You go with them. I'll bring Colt."

Maren cupped Colt's face and dropped another kiss on his lips. "I'll see you there. We need to talk."

He held on to her for a moment. "Yes, we do."

At the hospital, Maren stayed by her sister's side as she was rushed into an exam room. Haven drew stares from the staff and patients. The nails of her paws clicked on the linoleum floor.

A nurse hooked Opal up to oxygen, fitted her with a heart monitor as well as a monitor over the baby bump.

"The fetus's heartbeat sounds strong," thc nurse said.

Maren sent up a grateful prayer to know her baby niece or nephew would be okay.

The nurse started an IV drip. "You're what, five months along?"

"Yes, that sounds about right," Opal replied. "But I'm barely showing. Is that normal?"

Wanting to know the answer as well, Maren held her breath.

She had no idea what pregnancy should be like. She sent up a quick prayer that all would be well for Opal and the baby.

"Sometimes. We all carry our babies differently. The doctor will be in shortly to give you an exam and can better assess how you both are." The nurse patted Opal's hand. "Don't worry, Mama. I've been at this a long time. You and baby are good."

"Thank you, I needed to hear that," Opal replied.

So did Maren. She silently thanked God. As soon as the nurse left and they were alone, Opal said, "You and the DEA agent?"

"I hope so." A knot formed in Maren's chest. What would he say when they talked? Would he be open to hearing how she felt? Would he feel the same?

"What's your dog's name?" Opal asked, her gaze on Haven, who sat patiently by Maren's side.

"Haven."

"She did good today. That was some pretty scary stuff." Opal met her gaze. "You have a backbone of steel."

"Not really," Maren admitted. "Seeing you in danger and then knowing Colt got shot while saving us, it almost undid me." For a brief moment, she'd thought she'd lost him. The terror of a future without him had frozen her blood. She never wanted to feel that but it was a part of their lives and something they'd both have to contend with. The danger of their jobs would always be present but that didn't mean they couldn't enjoy every moment they had together. She wanted all the moments with him. And her sister and the little one growing inside of Opal.

"It would have undone me," Opal said. "You've always been the stronger of us."

"I think we're strong together. Promise me you won't ever disappear like that again," Maren said, her voice breaking. "When I thought you were dead…" She couldn't even express the pain, the grief she'd felt.

Regret flashed in Opal's eyes. "I'm sorry about that. I just thought it would be cleaner, and easier, for you."

She was filled with sadness, knowing Opal would think that way. "It's not. It never will be."

Guilt darkened Opal's eyes. "I thought, maybe, if you believed I'd drowned myself it would give you some closure. Unlike our parents' death."

Maren sucked in a breath. "No." But she understood how her drive to solve her parents' case had driven so much of their lives. That had to stop. "I'm working to let go of my need for closure. I must accept I won't get it in this life. But God knows and He will serve the justice that's deserved. I have to believe that. Because otherwise, I'll destroy any chance I have at happiness."

Opal held out her hand. Maren grasped it.

"I'm proud of you," Opal said. "Sisters are forever friends,"

Letting the tears fall, Maren nodded and repeated the phrase, "Sisters are forever friends. And soon an addition to our family. I can't wait to meet your child."

The beaming smile on Opal's face warmed Maren's heart. "I'm going to love this little one for all I'm worth. She, or he, will be blessed to have you as an aunt."

Pleased to be called aunt, Maren asked, "Have you thought of names?"

"Georgy if a boy or Georgina if a girl." The light in her eyes dimmed slightly and tears slipped down her cheeks. "My Georgy wanted so badly to be a father."

Maren squeezed her hand, her heart aching for her sister's loss. "You'll make sure your child knows they were loved by their daddy." Another thought occurred to her. "Hey, were you ever approached by a doctor wanting to send you to a free clinic? The guy has thinning red hair, a beard and wears silver eyeglasses."

Opal's head tilted. "No. What'd he do?"

Not wanting to upset her sister, Maren kept her expression neutral. "Nothing for you to worry about."

The curtain slid open, and the nurse stepped in, holding out a folded note. “Officer Anderson, this is for you.”

Maren unfolded the note to find Colt’s strong handwriting. The note read: *I’m in the lobby. C*

“Nurse, could you please send Agent Dawson back here?” Maren turned to Opal. “If you’re okay with that.”

Opal smiled despite the sadness lingering in her gaze. “Sure, since I have a feeling he’s going to become family, too.”

Hope spread through Maren’s chest. “From your lips to God’s ears.”

Colt and Rusk stood in the lobby of the emergency room with his SAC Leo Herman and the Colorado K-9 Unit task force leader, Emmett Dane. They’d just hammered out the fact that the Rocky Mountain DEA offices would need a new Deputy SAC, and Leo wanted Colt. Emmett had protested, wanting to keep him as part of the task force, but in the end, Colt made the tough decision.

As much as he wanted to stay partners with Maren on the task force, he wanted more to be her partner in life. He wasn’t sure doing both was in either of their best interests. Seeing her in danger had filled him with a kind of panicked fear he’d never experienced before. He’d been willing to do anything to protect her, even let Daniel go. Without a moment’s hesitation, he’d taken a bullet for her, which didn’t bode well if he wanted to stay alive while working with her. He’d get in her way with his need to protect and neither of them would be very effective at their jobs. Better to keep their professional careers separate from what he hoped would be a very close personal relationship.

Plus, the Rocky Mountain DEA office needed cleaning up. And he wanted to do it.

“As the DSAC,” Colt told Emmett, “I can still support the task force’s investigation.”

Emmett held out his hand. “I will take you up on that.”

"Agent Dawson?" The nurse to whom Colt had given a note for Maren returned. "Officer Anderson would like you to go to the exam room, if you can."

"Of course." Colt's gaze went to his SAC.

"Go on," Leo said. "Your duties will start when you're healed. Take what time you need. I'm glad you didn't suffer more than a bruised rib from taking a bullet practically point-blank."

So was Colt. The body armor had stopped the bullet from penetrating, but had left a nasty bruise on his rib.

He grinned at the older men. "Gentlemen, I've been summoned." A molten mix of anticipation and nervousness had him hurrying with Rusk at his side as he made his way back to where Maren and Haven waited outside an exam room.

"Is Opal okay?" he asked. "The baby?"

Looking to the door and then back at him, Maren answered, "Opal and baby are doing well. Or will be with some rest and nutrition. The doctor's examining them both now."

She took his hand and drew him down the hall to a secluded alcove. The dogs walked side by side and then sat with expectant gazes.

"What you did today…taking that bullet…" Her voice hitched and she took a shuddering breath. "I've never been so scared in my life."

"Hey, that's supposed to be my line," he said, squeezing her hands. "When I saw Daniel with his gun aimed at your head…" His throat tightened. "I almost lost it."

"As my sister says, scary stuff."

"Very scary, but part of the deal, right?" A flood of emotion crested in his chest. He'd come close to losing her today. They both had dangerous jobs; nothing in life was guaranteed. They had to grab what happiness they could in this life.

"Would you have really let Daniel go?" she asked.

"To save you? Yes. In a heartbeat. Though, to be honest, I

knew Emmett and the others were close. But I would have let Shadow run. I would, and will, do anything for you."

For a long moment, their gazes held. He remembered the way she'd kissed him. Was it just the heat of the moment? An action born out of adrenaline? He leaned toward her, wanting another kiss.

"Our cases aren't connected," she said, stopping his momentum.

He straightened. "No?"

"Opal never talked to Dr. Rolls," Maren said. "We'll keep searching for him."

"I've been asked to take on the position of deputy special agent in charge," he blurted, needing her to know.

Her eyes flared with surprise. "You're off the task force?"

"I can still assist as needed," he assured her just as he had Emmett. "But I think we're all better served if I accept this position."

"We won't be partners anymore."

Her sad tone had him flinching. "Not on the job." His heart rate doubled as he gathered her hands. "But maybe in life? What do you say? Could you take a chance on a guy like me?"

A different sort of surprise spread across her face. He wasn't sure if it was pleasure or not.

"I have a confession to make," she said softly.

Curious and a little wary because she hadn't answered his questions, he said, "I'm all ears."

She straightened and squared her shoulders. "What I said to you before about not wanting to be in a romantic relationship and not wanting to mess up our partnership—"

He held his breath. Where was this going? Was she going to reject him? They wouldn't be partners on the job now. Didn't that count for something?

"That was the old me," she said. "You and I make a great

team." Her teeth tugged on her lip. "Professionally and personally."

The moment of vulnerability raised goose bumps along his limbs. "What are you saying?"

"I've fallen in love with you, Colt Dawson."

Her words burst through him like a firework display on the Fourth of July. He brought her knuckles to his lips. The movement tugged at the bruise on his ribs, but he didn't care. "I'm so glad to hear you say that. Because I feel the same. I'm in love with you, Maren Anderson. And I will do everything I can to make sure that you know it every day of our lives."

A beaming smile spread across her face, and she threw her arms around him. Squeezing him tight. He groaned. And she jumped back. "Oh no. I hurt you."

He gathered her back in his arms a little more gently. "A hug from you could never hurt."

The door to the exam room opened and the doctor stepped out. "Opal would like to see you. We're about to do the ultrasound."

Colt stepped back. "I'll be here when you're done."

From inside the room Opal's voice could be heard, "You, too, Agent Dawson. And the dogs. I want the whole family here."

Colt's heart swelled with elation and love as he and Maren joined hands. With Rusk and Haven by each other's side, they stepped into the exam room for their first glimpse of the newest addition to their lives.

Lives that would be spent together.

* * * * *

If you enjoyed this story,
don't miss Protecting the Baby,
the next book in the
Colorado K-9 Unit series!

Discover all the books in this brand-new continuity:

Searching for the Truth *by Laura Scott*
Tracking the Taken Child *by Sharon Dunn*
Danger in the Rockies *by Terri Reed*
Protecting the Baby *by Jodie Bailey*
Fugitive Manhunt *by Sharee Stover*
Hunting an Arsonist *by Jessica R. Patch*
Uncovering Explosive Secrets *by Maggie K. Black*
Unraveling a Crime Ring *by Valerie Hansen*
Christmas K-9 Security *by Lynette Eason & Lenora Worth*

Available only from Love Inspired Suspense!

Dear Reader,

Thank you for taking this journey with Maren and Colt through the Rocky Mountains. I hope you enjoyed the twisty way they found each other. When writing, I try to imagine how I'd feel if I were put into the circumstances of my characters. While I don't have a twin or even a sister by blood, I do have many good friends whom I consider to be as close as a sibling, and the stress of knowing they might be in danger would be horrible.

Writing this story of Maren searching for her missing twin sister had me thinking about the ties that bind us to one another. Whether by blood or by choice, bonding to others is a part of being human and one of the gifts God has given us.

Though Maren had a hard time letting down her guard so that she could allow herself to love Colt, who had his own barriers up, the way these two characters interacted with each other came naturally and allowed the words to flow for me. They were a matched set for different reasons, but together they made a great team. Both in finding Maren's sister and bringing down the drug kingpin known as Shadow.

However, Mia Andrews is still missing and the criminals separating babies from their mothers need to be brought to justice. I hope you'll read the rest of the Colorado K-9 Unit series as more task force members work together to find the missing Mia and take down the illegal baby smuggling ring. You won't want to miss even one book.

Until next time, may you be blessed with love and joy.

Terri Reed